FOREVER CHERISHED

THE FOREVER SERIES
BOOK FOUR

AMANDA KIMBERLEY

For my pack Scott, Brittanny, Olivia, Sport, Onyx, and Luna

ACKNOWLEDGMENTS

In the grand scheme of the publishing world, writing is never an easy thing to do, but it is even harder to do the behind-the-scenes work for producing novels. I cannot thank the people enough that give me the support that is needed.

Thank you, Jessica, Karen, Paul, Carrie, Caryl, Paul, Dale, Steve, Jennifer, Deb, and Ronnie. You all are great cheerleaders and the only ones I can trust with my life—I mean WIPS!

Patience and Michelle, you have both been very supportive of my writing, as well and I thank you for your attendance to every social media event I've been involved with.

And, as always, I have to thank my first non-family member fan, Cheryl for not only being one but for also being a great friend.

I'm so glad you are all part of my pack!

ABOUT FOREVER CHERISHED

The bonds of passion should be cherished.

Have you ever felt like you were an animal living inside a human's body when it came to love?

The passion Keme has in his heart for the Fox and the opposing Sauk tribe may be blinded by what is right for Chepi if he cannot learn to control the beast from within.

The two tribes never really got along until Chepi and Keme gave them a reason to fight the pale-faced vampires together as one.

"Arnou died doing this, Matchitehew! We cannot stray this far from the village; that bear might get us too!" Keme spat with as much conviction as his diaphragm allowed.

"I understand you feel it is your duty to protect the entire tribe, but with all due respect, you are the chief's son and not the chief, Keme. Please relax! I am certain there's buffalo up this way. If we can get one, it will feed the entire tribe!"

"That is foolish pride talking, Matchitehew! We are better off hunting for deer because they are easier to find and lighter to carry!"

Matchitehew looked into Keme's cognac-colored eyes as if they would provide the vast wisdom he was seeking for the hunt they were embarking on. Many animals became scarce due to slow growth in vegetation. Their last three searches for food proved only meager offerings to their people.

"Perhaps you are right, Keme. It would be much harder to carry the buffalo on our own. And if we leave half of the buffalo in the elements, we run the risk of another animal taking off with our people's meal."

"Yes, that is exactly what I meant. Come, the deer were this way." Keme said as he turned on his heel.

The two ran swiftly through the forest, making sure to be light on their feet so as not to alert the deer of their presence. The sky was starting to darken as they approached a doe.

"Well, it's not what we expected, but it's something," Keme said as he reached for an arrow. He slid the bolt into the rest of the bow and quickly took aim. He released the bolt from his index finger and thumb, and the bolt hit the deer.

The two quickly ran towards the animal once it fell to the ground. Darkness was fast falling upon Keme and Matchitehew as they prepared the deer for transport.

"It is late. We will not make it back to the village tonight. Not with that bear still around. We should set up camp and travel on foot back to the tribe at dawn." Keme said to Matchitehew.

Matchitehew gathered some branches while Keme gathered rocks to start a fire. The two had the fire going and cooking a portion of the deer when a man approached them.

"Good evening." He said to the two.

"Good evening," Keme said.

"My name is Wisakachek, and I have lost my way from my tribe. It is now too dark for me to travel. Would you mind if I camp with you for the evening?"

"No, not at all. Please join us." Keme said.

"Thank you. I was going to try to press on, but I came across the delicious aroma of your dinner, and my stomach compelled me to stop. You see, I have been traveling for a few days and have not had luck finding anything to eat."

"There is a bear claiming much of the deer around here, I am afraid," Keme stated flatly. "But we can share some of ours."

"Do you have a little to spare for my tribe, as well? I was appointed to hunt, and like I said, it's been tough to find anything."

Keme did not want to give up the little meat they had for his tribe, but he was confident that his prayers to the gods would provide him with something by dawn. "Yes. We can share some of the food with you."

"But Keme?"

Since he understood full well what Matchitehew would say, Keme raised his hand to silence him before he continued. The stranger needed a sympathetic ear instead of a rude one. Keme's training to become the chief of the tribe taught him the patience to understand the difference.

The simple act of sharing their kill might help get the man to talk about where he had been hunting. The animals were showing signs of migrating to another water source. If Keme knew the stranger's direction, he could avoid hunting in those areas and focus on more fruitful ones.

Keme handed some of the meat to the man, who smiled and bowed. After some talk about his tribe, the man started to warm up to Keme's sympathetic ear and told Keme which areas he had already hunted in.

"Thank you for being so kind and telling us where you have already hunted. That will help us tomorrow when we go out again." Keme said while bowing his head to the stranger.

"It is I that would like to thank both of you. You are too kind. And in exchange for your kindness, I would like to offer a gift in return for the goodwill you have bestowed upon my people and me." Wisakachek said.

"A gift?"

"Yes. I'd like to offer you the power to hunt for your tribe without fearing being hunted yourself."

"And how do you propose that? Are you a magical medicine man or something?" Matchitehew chuckled.

"Something like that, yes." Wisakachek said with a smile as he continued, "I am the spirit god who is the guardian over an ancient and magical art known as shapeshifting."

"Shapeshifting? You mean like being able to change yourself into anything at will?" Keme inquired.

"Not exactly. The art of shapeshifting takes on the animal form of a wolf."

Keme's eyes widened.

"A wolf is a powerful creature! It can bring almost any animal to its knees! Maybe not the grizzly that has been giving us trouble, but a wolf is definitely a respectfully powerful animal. I could harness its power to feed my entire village! They would never go hungry again. That would be wonderful!"

"I would not be granting you the power of just any wolf. This wolf would be an enormous animal, and that grizzly would be no match for you."

"What a truly wonderful gift!" Matchitehew shouted.

"I will grant you this gift because of your kindness towards me, but I ask for one thing in return."

"And what is that?" Matchitehew asked.

"You can only hunt the animals you need to feed your village. You cannot harm anything more out of greed, and you most certainly can never use this power on a human being."

"I would not dream of ever doing that," Keme said.

Wisakachek nodded his head in agreement with Keme's statement. "You say that now but do not have the beast in you yet."

"What do you mean?"

"This gift is both good and evil, as well as pure and tainted simultaneously. Once you can understand the neutrality of this power, it will be easier to wield. Only then will you realize the strength of this wolf power. And there may be some times when you feel that this gift is stronger than your own being. But you cannot let that happen. You cannot hurt another human."

"I understand this, but that's not me. I would never hurt another human."

"Why don't the two of you sleep on this decision and tell me what you decide in the morning?"

"Okay, but I am certain my decision will not change," Keme said adamantly.

The three settle for the evening by watching the fire burn out. Keme was especially interested in watching the embers because the warmth made him appreciate Chepi, a beautiful girl he had met five moons ago while hunting for his tribe.

She was from the neighboring Sauk tribe and kept him company as they hunted that evening. Her hair's dark locks and lush eyes were a distraction while he was chasing game that night. But he did not care to admit that since they were just the warmth he needed tonight to decide whether to accept Wisakachek's gift.

Keme's initial reaction to accepting the wolf's power without hesitation all stemmed from wanting to please his father, the chief. He knew his father greatly missed his mother, and Keme tried to find ways for his father to be proud of him because of this.

His father respected hunting because it was a great responsibility to provide for the tribe. He learned all he could to be a great warrior and hunter to make his father proud. It is something he never took lightly. But something kept bothering him as he contemplated more of what Wisakachek said.

You say that now but don't have the beast in you yet.

Perhaps this god knew more about the powers of the wolf than Keme. He decided to do what Wisakachek suggested and sleep on the decision, especially for Chepi's sake since he greatly hoped she would be part of his future.

As he closed his eyes, an image of Chepi started to materialize within the depths of his mind.

"They must not learn about us yet," Chepi said

"Why?"

"Because they will not understand."

"But I love you, and I know that our tribes would unite with our love leading them. The gods would want this. They would never have the two of us fall in love with each other if our love was meant to be kept a secret."

"Keme, they don't know about your gift."

"What? Why haven't you told them? Especially now that animals are scarce in these parts! They need to know I can help!"

"And you need to calm down, Keme, before your temper gets the best of you again."

"My temper? I wouldn't be so mad if you would tell them! They need food!"

"Keme, please?" Chepi said as she stroked his arm. "I can't always be here to calm the beast within you. One day it may get the better of you just like it did Matchitehew."

"I will not let it get the best of me," Keme said while pounding his fist on the ground close to the campfire. The force was great enough to send a small half-burnt kindling twig into the air, and the kindling grazed Chepi's forearm. "Oh, Chepi!" Keme said as he tried to swipe the embers off of her arm.

"Stop! Don't touch me!"

"Chepi, I'm so sorry. I didn't mean to hurt you!"

"That's what I've been trying to tell you, Keme! That beast will one day get the better of you!"

Keme arose from the dream in a cold sweat. He placed his palms against his forehead and rubbed his cheeks while swallowing hard several times to try to quench the dryness in his throat.

"Do you still think the same as the night before?" Wisakachek asked.

"About the gift? Yes, yes, I do. About everything else that goes with it? Well, now I'm not so sure."

"Then this is truly a power you deserve to wield," Wisakachek said as he waved his hand before Keme and Matchitehew. "You see, it is more important that you understand that the gift is powerful rather than think you have to have the total understanding of how to wield it from the start. That knowledge of the wolf will come in time."

"But I am not ready. Please do not bestow this gift upon me. I may hurt someone. Someone that I care for deeply." Keme pleaded.

"It is already done. You have pleased the other gods and me, so we have decided to reward you." Wisakachek said. He then bowed to them both, turned on his heel, and walked into the thick of the forest. Within seconds he faded away into the scenery.

"What have I done?" Keme said as he buried his face in his hands.

"Keme, it will be fine! This power will be great for us! We can now feed the whole village! You'll see!" Matchitehew said while patting Keme on his shoulder. "I wonder how it works? Do you figure if we just think of a wolf?"

Within seconds of his lips speaking the word, Matchitehew's mouth and nose elongated until they transformed into a wolf's snout. He then beat his chest and got on all fours before his backside transformed into a dog-like state. His skin grew a thick coat of fur the color of burnt umber, and his whiskey-brown eyes became saffron-colored yellow.

"Matchitehew! What happened to you?"

"*Nothing happened to me, Keme. What are you talking about?*" Keme could not hear him speak but understood his words in thoughts.

"But you're a — "

"*Wolf?*"

"Yes!"

"*Oh, how wonderful! Keme! Go on! See if you can! All you have to do is think of a wolf, and you will become one!*"

"It's that easy? Just think of a wolf?"

Keme contemplated for a long minute about wolves. He had encountered many in his hunting experience, but the most gorgeous was an eerie black-colored one. Keme noticed the creature almost 50 moons ago. It was regal standing on a cliff that connects to the mountain near the waterfall catching the rays of the moonlight. That gorgeous soul remained forever engrained in Keme's memory.

Within seconds of thinking of that wolf, Keme

felt his stomach churn. A sharp pang slid up from his abdomen towards his lungs. Keme beat his chest similarly to Matchitehew, hoping to press out the pain coming over him. His knees buckled, and he fell to the ground with a need to get on all fours.

His mouth and nose elongated into a snout like Matchitehew, but Keme's cognac eyes changed to a royal yellow. Ebony-colored fur started to grow from his skin, and his back elongated into a large, lean mass.

"Wow, Keme! You are larger than me as a wolf!"

"That is because I made him a dire wolf, Matchitehew."

They both sensed Wisakachek's voice but could not see him, which could only mean that they both possessed the power of telepathy. Keme's tail wagged with excitement at discovering one of his newfound powers. He then howled at the eagerness to find more of his abilities as a wolf.

"Remember, this power is great. You must only use it for hunting animals, and never humans. And you must never share this power with a mortal." Wisakachek said.

"Share with a mortal? But aren't we mortals? And how could we share this power since a god gave it to us?" Keme retorted in a confused state.

Wisakachek did not reply telepathically, so Keme tried to voice his concerns in speech but found he could only howl out the confusion that Wisakachek placed upon him.

"Keme, why does that matter? We understand what this gift is for, so let's find food for the village." He heard Matchitehew saying in the back of his mind.

Keme shook his head and backside, trying to free the confusion from him, and followed Matchitehew deep within the forest.

The trees and brush seemed to come alive in a way Keme had never seen before. The colors of the leaves, bugs, and even the dirt were brighter and more vivid, almost surreal in nature. What he noticed and appreciated as a human paled in comparison to the beauty he was discovering as a wolf.

His snout detected more vibrant fragrances in the flowers and a vile odor of a decaying carcass. Every one of his five senses seemed to be heightened in wolf form. As he continued to press his snout to the more defined scent of the earth, he came across the distinct stench of a bear nearby. Keme motioned to Matchitehew to move towards the left, and with that, the two came upon a stream where a grizzly bear was hunting for salmon.

They both crouched quietly to not alarm the bear of their presence. And when the two were ready, they pounced upon it. Keme went for the jugular, while Matchitehew went for the chest. The grizzly fell limp within a minute of the battle. When the bear looked as if it would no longer move, the two returned to human form as if it were common instinct to do so.

"How are we going to get it home to the village? We are human again, and this thing weighs a ton." Matchitehew said.

"It shouldn't be hard if we both carry it. I'll pick it up by the back and you the front." Keme said as he raised the back part up off of the ground with ease. "See? This should be easy. And besides, the village is not far from here. Maybe a mile at the most in that direction."

Matchitehew's face looked amazed as he picked up the front of the bear.

"You are right. This shouldn't be difficult at all. We must also have the wolf's strength in our human form."

"We must."

The two were back in the village in minutes and greeted with cheers. The elders of the tribe started a sacred fire, and the whole tribe danced in celebration of their prayers being answered through Keme and Matchitehew.

TWO

The celebrations ended in the early evening. A large smile grew on Keme's face as he watched his father beat his chest in pride and dance in the sacred circle with the elders. He noticed Keme sitting on a nearby log and walked over to him.

"I am proud of you, my son. You have done well for the tribe. You are a great hunter and warrior for this tribe and will surely please the gods by being a great chief."

"Thank you, Father," Keme said as he got up from the log.

"Go and get some rest so you can hunt again in the morning at first light."

"I will," Keme said as he turned towards his teepee.

He stared at it for a few moments before

deciding on a stroll through the forest, thinking it was the best way to reward himself on the excellent hunt and the only way to get a glimpse of the girl, Chepi that appeared in his dreams nightly.

As he headed out, he looked up at the sky. A habit his father taught him to help direct him back home. Tonight, however, he was using the lesson for something else. He remembered meeting Chepi near a large rock that the Chief Star showed directly upon and hoped she'd be there since he yearned to meet up with her again.

Chepi came up upon him before he realized how close he was following the Chief Star. He grew quick to silence his steps towards her just in case she wished to be alone.

She was stark in the moonlight and knelt praying with her spear in hand. Keme was in awe of her beauty and devotion. He did not want to interrupt her, but his body moved despite his mind.

"Who is that?"

"It is I, Keme."

"Keme? Oh! How I have missed you! It has been 6 moons since we saw each other last. I figured you grew tired of me."

"No, I didn't! I hunted for my tribe, and it took longer than expected."

"I understand. My tribe is having the same problem. We have found very little in 8 moons. I'm worried for the youngest of the tribe, as well as the elders, and have prayed for us to find a feast. Would you care to pray with me?"

"You do not need to pray to the gods anymore for this. I will help you."

"Really? Will you? But? Who are you to help? You understand my father only looks to certain warriors to hunt for our tribe. Unfortunately, he has never looked upon the Fox tribe favorably."

Keme surmised himself to be the last person Chepi's father would want help from. Her father and his had never gotten along since Keme could remember. Keme's father never told him why and he never pushed, but Keme couldn't bear to see Chepi and her people go hungry over a spat between their fathers.

"I believe that the gods think I should help your tribe, and so should you." He said with a wink. "How much do you need for your tribe? A deer, buffalo, or bear?"

She looked at him with a furrowed brow.

"You cannot handle anything but a deer on your own."

"I can handle anything that you need for your tribe. Please have faith in me, Chepi. The gods do."

"Fine then. We will need a buffalo."

* * *

Chepi stated it, but she had been tracking the buffalo and spotted them retreating farther south from the tribes' locations. None of the hunters in her tribe seemed to notice that all the animals were following the buffalo's lead. Nor did any notice that the vegetation grew sparse near both villages with each passing moon. It had become painfully evident to Chepi that the tribes would have to move again so the hunters could forge a trip in a shorter amount of time.

"It is not a problem. Do you need one or two?" Keme asked her, breaking her train of thought.

"One or two? As in buffalos? Why would you say that?"

"It's been a while since I've ever visited your people. We must have been babes the last time our fathers spoke to one another. I am unsure of how large your tribe is now, and I want to ensure I hunt for the right amount for your people."

"Ah, one should suffice."

Chepi narrowed her eyes, trying to understand how a man could be so bold, but she had heard the rumors. Keme found a bear for his tribe to feast on earlier that day, and she hoped he could also provide a similar miracle for her. She then winked at Keme and hoped he answered her prayers.

"I will get you what you need. You do not need to pray any longer." Keme said as he put his hands on her shoulders.

"Oh, but I do! You know that I am the chief's daughter. It is my duty to do so."

"Your duty is done for today. Your prayers have

been answered." He said as he stroked gentle circles on her shoulders with his thumbs.

Chepi closed her eyes to take in his touch and commit it to memory. "But how are you going to do this, Keme? You are but one man, for one thing, and for another, you are from the one village that my father hates. How can you answer this prayer for my tribe and me?"

She lowered her head slightly, which was within inches of his bare chest. Keme's breath hitched as she placed her hands on his chest. "You know I want nothing more than for our fathers to get along, but I fear that mine chooses not to and would never accept a bountiful gift from you. Even if you do manage to get a buffalo." She said as she buried her face in his exposed chest.

Keme stroked her hair with his hand and tried hard not to let his emotions toward her get the best of him, but the more he took in her sweet floral scent, the more his wolf grew excited. "This spot we keep meeting at is near your people?" He asked as he lightly stroked the braids in her hair once more.

"Yes."

"Meet me back here just before dawn. I will provide enough for your people, and you don't have to tell your father that it came from me."

"How can you provide for your village and ours in that short time? You would have to be a god."

"I am not a god, Chepi, but like I said, they favor me."

"I am not so sure about that," Chepi said with a smirk.

"Just humor me for now, and you will see at dawn," Keme said as he lowered her hands from his chest.

"Okay, I will meet you here at dawn."

Chepi had little hope that Keme could provide for all of her people but fought violently within her mind for faith in him to come back with something suitable. She started to grow fond of him and yearned for the time to pass quickly so she could see him again, even if he returned empty-handed.

There was no denying her feelings for Keme any longer, especially after she prayed to the gods. She was falling for him and could no longer deny her heart. All she could do now was have faith that the gods found a way to make Keme's hunt bountiful enough to win her father's grace.

* * *

Keme kissed the back of Chepi's hand and fled into the forest to find a big enough bounty for her tribe. Once he was confident that he was out of her sight, he took to his wolf form to better track the animals with his keen snout. A buffalo's scent rushed through his nostrils an hour into the hunt. He crouched in his wolf-like position, intent on killing the giant beast, and then sprang up it with a quick hit to its side. The buffalo put up a decent fight, but it ended with a swift blow to the animal's jugular.

He carried the prey through the woods on his back and grew impatient, waiting to gaze upon Chepi's expression, seeing his hunt for her in tow. The sun was just about to creep over the horizon when he noticed her walking through some brush, and he quickly turned back into human form just before their eyes met.

"My eyes must be deceiving me!" Chepi said as she ran towards Keme. "You really did it! The gods do favor you! Oh, thank you, Keme!" She said as she looked down at the buffalo. She then gazed back into his eyes. It was the first time he saw how beautifully lush they were in the light of the morning. They boasted a bounty as abundant as the leaves in the forest during the summer. She put her hand on his chest. "How can I ever repay you for this?"

Keme's eyes widened slightly as he took a slight step backward. When she first put her hands on his yesterday, he didn't expect it, but he assumed she was touching him for comfort. He never expected her to do it again. Electric heat shot through his body, and his wolf howled within him. No other woman had ever caressed him like that before. His mother died giving birth to him; therefore, he knew little about a woman's touch and what it would do to him.

To feel any kind of gentleness from the opposite sex was something almost foreign to him, yet he didn't want her to stop. Her eyes darted away from him, and he realized that hurt him more than it should.

"You talk like I am a warrior who saved you in battle. I did nothing warrior-like today. I merely hunted for a village. Any hunter can do what I did." Keme said as he stepped back towards her and reached for her hand. He hoped that gesture would allow him the courtesy of stealing another glimpse of her beautiful green eyes.

"The buffalo have eluded my people for weeks. We figured the animal's spirit to be too great for us to hunt, yet the creature was no match for you. If you do not wish to call yourself a great warrior, can I at least call you a great hunter, then?" Chepi asked as she stepped closer to him. Her gaze was still towards the ground.

Keme, sensing the touch of her buckskin dress against his bare chest, yearned for another view of Chepi's eyes. Before he could catch his movements, he found his hand touching her chin to raise it, so her eyes met his. The early light from the sun danced upon her eyes, and Keme wanted nothing more than to get lost in that vast green forest of mystery. As he smiled, he stroked her cheek.

"If you are compelled to call me a great hunter, then I can accept that, but only if it pleases you to say such a thing." He said as he wrapped his arms around her waist and drew her closer to his chest.

"It pleases me." She said as she palmed his cheek.

Keme closed his eyes and twisted his head in search of the palm of her hand, and he pressed on it gently. Drawing her lips towards his, he brushed them for a brief moment before the sound of a branch snapped, startling them both. "I think she must be this way. Chepi? Are you here?"

Chepi abandoned Keme's embrace, "It is my uncle. Come! We must show him your hunt to bring it back to the village."

"Are you sure that will be alright? I thought we were keeping this from your father?" Keme said, trying to hide the fluster in his voice.

"Uncle! I am here! Look! Keme from the Fox tribe has given us a gift!"

"Is that so?" the uncle said as he came into full view. His hair was thick and as dark as his voice. His midnight-colored eyes also matched that darkness.

"Yes! It is a buffalo, and I can help you bring him back to your village." Keme said while planting his feet firmly on the ground. Grounding himself always helped him to gain the confidence and composure he needed when facing another man.

"No. That is okay. We can take it from here." The uncle said abruptly while slightly pushing Keme aside. "Chepi, you should get back to the village.

Your father is looking for you." The uncle did not take his eyes off Keme.

Keme lowered his head as the uncle walked past him. Since the Sauk tribe never got along with his Fox tribe, he did not want to push them further away, but he found it difficult to remain silent now that he knew he had fallen for Chepi. The hunt, at least he hoped, would be the peace offering the two tribes needed to coexist together. It would be hard for Keme to be accepted by Chepi's family because of the bad blood between both chiefs, but Keme truly wished to try.

He looked at Chepi's uncle, wishing for a sign that the small offering was a step in the right direction. Perhaps if it were, he'd gain the ability to woo the Sauk chief's daughter. The uncle's gaze met Keme squarely after looking at the buffalo. The man got up from the fresh kill and walked closer to Keme.

"I know this offering was of your own accord and not that of your father. It is good you have become a great man. You are probably greater than your father could ever aspire to be, but please," the uncle put his hand on Keme's shoulder before he continued, "may I give you a word of advice? No offers you give to the Sauk Chief will mend the great rift between our people. Chepi is his only daughter and very precious to him since she is now all he has." The uncle said. He took a deep breath through his nose. His nostrils flared out before he continued.

"The chief will not take kindly to a gesture construed as curry favoring his daughter. Strongbow will regard this as foolishness on your part."

"But that was never my intention." Keme pleaded.

"It may not be your intention, but I know you and she has grown fond of one another. And you, my boy, are young. Arrogance is a trait that is deeply embedded in youth. And it runs rampant with the Fox tribe elders as well."

"But that is not my intention. It never was. You have to believe me! I merely want to use my gift to help the tribes I come across."

"We have heard the story of your great hunt. It traveled through your village and to ours fast. But keep in mind you will only be in favor of the gods for so long. Please, do yourself and your heart a favor, and find a girl to love among the Fox tribe. I can assure you that would be a far happier outcome than this."

Keme lowered his head again and walked past Chepi's uncle. There was no point in arguing further on the issue because he knew the uncle would never change his mind.

As Keme continued to walk through the forest toward his tribe, he thought about Chepi and how close her body was to him. Her curves were perfectly intertwined against his, and Keme wished he could see the malachite of her eyes glisten under the moonlight once more. They were perfect in the light of day and even more exquisite at night.

He had hoped for a longer kiss before they came across her uncle. A pang welled up in his lower belly as he tried to appreciate her lips' taste, knowing he might never taste them again. And then, a sharp pain replaced the pang.

Keme grabbed his stomach in protest as he fell to the ground.

It is the beast within you. You must control it!

A voice he assumed was his self-conscious uttered, and he tried to obey the command. The sharp pain was the wolf trying to emerge, and he would not let it come to the forefront of his mind. He had to harness its power to control this beast if he had any hope of making sure his dream of Chepi would never come to fruition.

The pain traveled up through his chest, and he tried to beat the pain out of his chest, but the pain seemed to split open his chest. He let out a howl; within seconds, he was the wolf. Keme ran back towards the thickness of the forest to clude the Sauk tribe as best as he could.

As he came upon a clearing near the river, patchouli touched his snout as his gaze shifted towards the direction of the scent, and that is when his eyes met hers for the second time that day. His heart felt like it was about to stop. He could not let her see him like this and quickly tried to run behind a large rock to block her view of him, but he was too late.

"Keme, I know it is you, and I am not afraid. Please, come out."

He had hoped to pass himself off as just another wolf in the forest, but he was much larger than any of the regular wolves and was now caught, having little choice. Keme either had to face her as the beast he became, thanks to Wisakachek, or try to find a way to change back. As he decided on the latter, Keme waited by the rock for the transformation to occur. Strangely, the wolf refused to change back until he saw her within full view.

THREE

Chepi came face to face with the eyes of a wolf as she turned a corner down the wooded path leading back to her village. It was the most enormous wolf she had ever seen in all her years on earth. His fur was midnight black, and his eyes were a regal, royal yellow. As she met the wolf's gaze, the eyes softened into a familiarity. They belonged to Keme, and there was no mistaking it.

She heard the rumors that the gods had bestowed a unique gift upon him, and now she had proof that he was no ordinary hunter. She recognized by his hesitation that he did not want her to see him in this state, but she found it hard to restrain herself from running toward him.

Keme plagued all of her thoughts during the walk home to the village. Kissing him was all she could think about and had wanted to do since she left Keme with her uncle. She ached to talk with him about her growing feelings toward him and find out if she might have mistaken the kiss for something more. She was grateful to him for hunting for her tribe, and her appreciation could have been thought of as just that. An ache in her lower abdomen compelled her to discover if he, too, wanted her as much as she wanted him.

As she ran over to him, she witnessed him change back to his human form as quickly as the blink of her eyes. He lay clad on the rock. A flush of heat came upon her cheeks as she caught a glimpse of his shaft before he covered it. She lowered her head.

"I am sorry. I did not mean to—it's just that I wanted to see you." She managed to mumble as she darted her eyes from him toward the ground that was dangerously close to his manhood. She tried not to glare at his hands but found it hard not to do so. Never had she seen something so gorgeous and enormous, and thoughts of her womanhood encompassing his mammoth rod ravaged her down to her core.

"No, Chepi. It is okay. Just give me a second." Keme said as he reached for the nearest brush. When he found a sufficient amount, he fashioned it into an undergarment to cover his front and backside.

"I SHOULD NOT BE HERE."

Keme's heart sank as Chepi's words stung his ears.

"Why?"

"You, you, are not decent." She said as her eyes trailed to the brush barely covering him. "You, uh, must be uncomfortable."

"I am fine. All you did was startle me to the point of me forgetting to shift closer to where I left my clothes."

"I should leave you be, then, so you can do that."

"No, don't go! Please stay here with me for a while?" He said as he motioned her to sit next to him on the rock.

"All right. I will, but I must admit, this isn't exactly how I thought our next meeting would be."

"Nor I," Keme said with a chuckle. "But I'm glad you are here," Keme caressed her cheek with his hand and drew her closer to him. "Because if you were not here, I wouldn't be able to do this."

He drew his lips towards hers, and she felt an electric heat overcome her body before settling deep within her belly. She moaned over his lips as her hands explored every inch of his exposed body.

Her lips felt like the petals of a wildflower, delicate and soft. Keme reached for her torso to pull her closer to him, hoping to savor every inch of her lips and the gorgeous curves of her body. Drunk with her taste, his mouth traveled down her chin and neck before it settled around her collarbone. He indulged in more of her delicacy before she let out a soft moan. He nuzzled into her flesh with his nose in response to her pleasure.

Chepi's hand caressed his chest and slid toward the brush covering him. She removed the leaves and grabbed his shaft, stroking it from the tip to the base. Keme, now entirely under her influence, did not rebut her straddling him. In fact, he welcomed it.

Her eyes were verdant, almost as if they were burning for him. Drunk with desire, his hands slinked up her waist and encompassed her breasts. He stroked her nipples through the fabric until his manhood hardened with passion, causing him to loosen the wrap of her dress to expose her chest so his thumbs could experience the nakedness of her chest. She began to rock against his shaft in retort.

Keme let out a moan of pleasure before his

hands wrapped around her waist to guide her up and down his shaft as it grew with desire for her inner lips to wrap around him. He kissed every inch of her face as she continued to grind his member perfectly.

"I want to be yours, Keme." She said in an almost inaudible tone.

Keme smiled as the words tickled his ear, but the words that escaped his lips were, "Oh, Chepi!" The ache in his underbelly wanted nothing more than to cultivate her as he guided her center onto his sex.

The pang then grew into a sharp pain. He clutched his belly because he knew the transformation would come. Desperately hoping to squelch the beast within him, he pushed Chepi off him to pound his chest, desperately hoping the gesture would make his wolf submit to his command.

No! This can't happen now! He found himself almost pleading with his wolf.

"Keme, focus on the love you have for Chepi. That is the only way to control the beast."

Wisakacheck, is that you? But how can I hear you right now?

"We will always be connected. I kept that link to help you in times of need with the gift."

Keme let out a cry of pain.

"Focus, Keme. Focus! It is the only way to save you and her!"

Keme grappled with the pain traveling toward his chest.

"No!"

"I am so sorry, Keme. I should not tempt you like this." Chepi said as she got up and started to adjust herself.

"Chepi, no! I didn't mean for you to stop."

"It's alright, Keme. You are right. We should not be doing this. Our tribes are in great peril with the animals' migration period. And our tribes need to heal before we ever try forcing a union between us upon them. I am so sorry for letting my feelings overcome my head."

"But Chepi, that's not it. That's not what's happening with me right now."

"No. I am the chief's daughter. I should not let my heart rule my head. You are too kind to allow me to continue this foolishness."

"Chepi, that's not what I mean." He said as he clutched his chest once more and let out a long breath. His body started to calm, allowing him to learn the grounding that Wisakachek was telling him about. His strength to control the beast was found in his love for Chepi. He knew that now. The beast subsided within him, and his head was clear enough to talk to her.

"Can I talk now?"

"Yes." She said as she lowered her head and knelt beside him.

He raised her gaze up to his eyes with his thumb and index finger. "That's better for two reasons. One, I like talking with my equals and not down on them. And two, I like seeing those pretty eyes of yours." Her face softened with each of his words. "Chepi, I was not saying no to you. Not in the least bit. I want nothing more than to be with you."

"There's a but coming, though. I can feel it."

Keme gave her a sheepish smile. "Hardly! I screamed no at myself."

"I do not understand."

"You now understand that the talk amongst our tribes is true. I can hunt for the tribes as a dire wolf, but this power is two-fold. I have a beast within me that I must learn to control for the sake of us all."

"You seem to able to handle containing this beast on some level. You changed back when I ran to you."

"How can you say that with so much conviction?"

"Because I know the beast is not before me, you are. That is how I have such conviction."

"You seem so sure."

"Yes. I am."

"But how?"

"Because the gods would not have me here with you if it was not safe to be."

"And again, how can you say this with so much conviction?"

"I prayed for you two moons before I met you, and the thunder gods answered those prayers by sending you to me."

"You have so much faith in the gods. I have a lot to learn from you." He said as he stroked her cheek and chin.

"It would be my honor to do so, Keme."

He cupped her cheek and drew her lips close to his.

"We should stop, though." She said as she was tenderly kissing him on his lips.

"You are right. We should." He said as he continued to feather her lips with light kisses, not wanting to part from the warmth of her embrace.

"I am serious!" She said as she continued to kiss his mouth and left cheek.

"But how serious can you be if you still kiss me?" he said with a sheepish grin.

"Very serious." She gave him a quick peck before rising to her feet. "Come, let us find out where the animals are traveling, so we save both tribes." She said while reaching for his hand.

"Um, why don't you start without me, and I'll catch up?" Keme said as he gestured towards his naked body. "I'll need to grab my clothing first." Heat rushed to his cheeks.

"Oh! Right!" Chepi's cheeks were starting to match his color. "I'll just start ahead. Good idea."

"I will find you shortly, I promise," Keme said

with a wink. It would not be hard to find where he tossed his clothing. The wolf's power had now given him a keen sense of smell, but the thought of even that power had Keme realizing his nightmare of hurting Chepi could come true.

He had to find a guaranteed way of holding the beast at bay. It was his only chance to keep Chepi in his life. He knew he had little chance to win the graces of her father and tribe, but if he could not control the beast, they'd never allow their union.

Zhang! Of course! Why didn't I think of him sooner!

Keme's father befriended a medicine man many moons back named Zhang.

This man might be my only chance to have Chepi in my life.

"What you seek is not difficult, but it can be hard to maintain, Keme. You are new to your powers, and the focus you would need to control the beast within you is advanced training."

"I am willing to learn, Zhang. And you know I have no choice!"

"Yes. It is unfortunate about Matchitehew."

"He was such a good man. A great warrior! How could he allow the beast to overcome him and kill a human? It's not in his nature to hurt anyone, especially those he greatly respects. Matchitehew hunted side by side with Cochise since they were old enough to handle spears. This is my fault. I should have been with him instead of with Chepi." Keme said as he pounded his fist on Zhang's rosewood altar table.

"Keme, this is not your fault! Matchitehew was the one that chose his destiny. Not you."

"But now, because of him, my destiny is being written for me. They will kill me if they find out that I can shift too. Or worse! They might go after Chepi to get to me! I have to protect her!"

"Keme, understand that I will do everything possible to help you and her. Where is she now? Still following the trail of the animals for food?"

"No. We had already found the new water source that the animals are using. We were near the villages when we found out what Matchitehew had done. She should not be that far behind. I told her to meet us here."

"All right. Well, let's not waste any more time. Come! We need to gather herbs for this spirit walk!"

Zhang led Keme around the back of his cottage. The house would have seemed out of place among all the teepees, but it was hidden deep in the densely wooded area of the forest close to a waterfall. Zhang loved the sound of water, which is why he chose the spot to call home.

They heard rustling from their left as they gathered the sage and lavender.

"Chepi? Is that you?"

"Yes, my love, I am here. I am afraid I cannot stay for long. There is talk in the villages that they will be hunting Matchitehew and you."

"I was afraid of this, and for your safety. Chepi, you cannot return to them."

"I am the daughter of the Chief of the Sauk tribe. It is my duty to go back."

"And I am the son of the Chief of the Fox tribe and understand your duty well. But I don't want to lose you. You mean far too much to me."

"Let's talk about this later. We have little time. Come!" Zhang interrupted.

He led them both to a small clearing near the waterfall and a cave. They went into the cave. It was dank and dark until Zhang waved his hand over a makeshift fire pit.

"For this to work well, you must allow the spirit to enter you without resistance. Do you understand?"

"Yes," Keme said as he sat cross-legged by the fire.

"Close your eyes. I sense that our time is scarce to perform this spirit walk. They are coming for you soon."

"What are we going to do?" Chepi asked.

"I can convince them that Keme will cause no harm. But he cannot be disturbed while he's doing the spirit walk. We will have to stall the tribes when they get here."

Keme closed his eyes and put his palms upright on each knee. Zhang lit the bundled herbs and smudged Keme. Within a few minutes, Keme was in a trans-like state.

"It has started. Keme will be fine now while he talks to the spirit Wisakachek. Let's prepare for both tribes."

"Are you sure he will be okay?"

"For now. But we must get to both tribes, or Keme won't be."

They rushed through the forest and brush to get to the front of Zhang's cottage and were greeted by the tribes as they came through the clearing on the opposite side.

"Chepi, what are you doing here? It is not safe, my child. You must go back to the village. Two beasts walk among us and must be dealt with before anyone else dies."

"I am fine, Father." She said while motioning towards Zhang.

"We are hunting dangerous animals, and with all due respect to Zhang, it is still not safe for my daughter to be here! You are the Chief's daughter and have responsibilities to the tribe in my absence."

"With all due respect, Father, my responsibilities to the tribe are better served here and right now."

"Go home and let me handle this."

"Father! I am no longer a child!"

"By talking like this in front of our people, I question that."

Chepi clenched her fists as her father looked down on her. She knew it was not her place to question her father, but if the Chief had his way, he would be killing the only person that could save both tribes from starvation.

"Do you know which direction we need to travel for food, Father?"

"That is not my concern or yours at this— "

"Do you, Father? Answer me!"

"No. I do not." Strongbow said with a condescending sigh.

"Do you know how we can hunt for food while our village migrates toward a better food source?"

"No. Not at this— "

"Then you have no right to question me, Father. My place is here. I intend to do what is right for our people."

"If I may ask, what do I owe this visit to my home?" Zhang interrupted as he stepped between the two of them.

"We are tracking a couple of beasts, Zhang, and we believe that one is somewhere around your home," Strongbow said as his lips thinned.

"Well, that is impossible."

"How can you say that with such certainty?"

"Because I am justified in my certainty, Chief Strongbow."

"Not today."

"Oh yes, yes I am today. You cannot take Keme!

That boy is being taught by me, and he will remain here until his lessons are learned."

"I see." the Chief said as he lowered his head.

He knew full well that arguing with Zhang would do him little good. There were rules about the cultivation of a creature's powers, and Zhang, as a neutral sorcerer, had been granted the ability to train such beings by the gods. Strongbow lowered his clenched fists admitting defeat.

"Very well. Let us let Zhang tend to his student."

Everyone started to leave.

"Father?"

"Yes?"

"Why are you allowing this? You aren't fighting back as I expected you to."

"Zhang will be able to help control the beast within Keme. I am certain of that. And besides, it is common law that Zhang be allowed to train any magical being before its fate is decided."

"Father?" she said as she rushed to him. "I need you to understand why I am here."

The Chief stroked his daughter's hair.

"I more than understand."

"Do you?"

"Darling, I was young once too. I can understand that your heart led you here. But I also understand that your head did too. It is noble to think that our tribes can coexist together." Chief Strongbow said. His eyes trailed off towards the right. "It is more than noble, and it just might work."

"What do you mean, Father?"

"I did not want to discuss this with either of you because it might be nothing, but the moon and star gods keep me up at night."

"The visions again, Father?"

"Yes. And this time, I can see the visions more clearly. There are beings with stark white features. They almost appear to be the dead who walk among the living. They come to destroy our people, land, and food sources. They are strong and powerful, my darling, stronger than any mortal I have ever met."

"They are not human, are they?"

"No. And these beings may be more beastly than Keme and Matchitehew could ever dream of being."

"Your visions of these magical creatures are accurate. I have seen them too." Zhang said as he stroked his long gray beard.

"Zhang, we cannot allow them to exist any longer. They are a threat far greater than the beast, Keme, that is contained on your leash."

"Perhaps Keme can help us with these creatures?"

"Perhaps he can."

"I will continue to work with Keme and study our visions further. There must be a way for us to drive these creatures off of the land before they destroy us all."

Keme to flourished under Zhang's guidance. He grew more powerful to hunt every day and yet, controlled the beast within him enough to shapeshift at will. Zhang's only fear as he continued to train Keme was how calm Keme might be if provoked. All men lose their patience every once in a while, but if Keme did, it could prove deadly.

After several moons, Zhang's visions of the immortals reaching their unchartered soil grew clear. He feared a battle between the shapeshifters and the immortal vampires was imminent. Zhang started to teach Keme martial arts to protect the tribes but wondered if Keme had the strength to change back to human form after a fight with the immortals. Chepi's life, along with the rest of the tribes', hung solely on Keme's will.

"Can't you let me practice with her now? I am certain I'm ready; if I'm not, I know you will keep her safe." Keme pleaded.

"I'm not certain if the time is right yet, Keme."

"You said that these vampires are coming here soon. If I do not start trying to control the beast in front of the ones I love, I will be of no use to you should we battle with these immortals."

Zhang glanced at Keme's cognac-colored eyes and, for the first time, witnessed the wisdom growing within them. He put his hand on Keme's right shoulder.

"You are right. We should test your powers out. I will get Chepi and Chief Strongbow."

* * *

Keme found himself pacing while Zhang traveled to get them. He wasn't sure if he was right in deciding to see Chepi and wondered if seeing his father first would have been a better idea. Zhang did agree to it, but now Keme's body was trembling with the fear that he may have persuaded Zhang a little too quickly.

Keme rubbed the back of his head and continued to pace as he contemplated his decision to see her further. A warm tingle started to flow through his body as he remembered the last time they were together. He longed to hold her close to him once more. He closed his eyes, knelt down, and gathered enough muster within him to do the one thing he hadn't done since meeting Chepi, pray.

I am never big on praying, Wisakachek, but if there was ever a time that I needed your guidance with this beast, it is now.

A calmness surrounded Keme, and he attributed it to Wisakachek answering his prayer.

Keme could hear the brush rustling in the distance, and then he caught the scent of patchouli tickling his nose. The close proximity of her made his extremities twinge and burn with excitement.

He tried to suppress this excitement so as not to awaken the beast, but something strange and unexpected happened. He found that the closer she got to him, the calmer he became. There was little need for him to perform the Tai Chi that Zhang taught him. When he caught a glimpse of her charcoal black hair and green eyes, her father also quickly came into view. The scowl on the chief's face made Keme take a step back.

"So I take it that you feel you are ready to be around humans again?" Chief Strongbow said with a sternness that became pronounced in his tightening jawline. His brows furrowed as he hissed, "Just understand that I don't think I can ever trust you, especially when it comes to Chepi."

Zhang saw the growing tension between the two thicken in the air. He had always tamed squabbles within the magical realms, but he did not know how to tame the emotions of a mortal father. The tension between the two had very little to do with magic, but as a father figure to many, he found himself wanting to step in between them. "Yes, well, let's get on with it. Shall we?" Zhang interrupted. "I'm sure you can understand the importance of this since the immortals are fast approaching us."

As Zhang instructed, Chief Strongbow and his daughter tried to provoke Keme into shifting, but nothing seemed to anger him enough to turn into his wolf. Zhang motioned for Chepi and Strongbow to step back and then signaled for Keme to shift upon his command. Keme finally shapeshifted and stood clad in his dire wolf form.

Zhang then motioned for Chief Strongbow and Chepi to step closer to Keme to try to get him to succumb to the wolf form, but Keme remained docile in his wolf form. Not even a growl came from his throat. Zhang motioned again for Keme to change back, and he did without hesitation.

"It does appear you are ready for battle, Keme." Chief Strongbow said while nodding in approval. "How long do you think we have before the vampires arrive?"

Zhang pointed to the sky and said, "We have until the next moon."

The land was foreign to them as they twisted and turned through the thickest parts of the forest. The ground struck their feet hard, having little give to it like their Mother Country. They attributed this to the lack of rain they experienced in the few days they had arrived. England was always so moist and dank. A proven perk to hunting their prey since the thick air made it easy to slip in and out of the shadows.

"We have not seen one mortal since we left the docks in London, Lilith."

"I am certain we will come across some soon, Drake. There are rumors that these humans are savages, and no one should miss them or track our killing of them back to our kind. We can live here for a century or two undetected!" She said to Dracula as she stroked his cheek with the back of her hand.

"Let's hope you are right and we come across some soon, or we may have no choice but to dine on the deer."

"Stop with such foolish talk and learn to trust me. I love you and will always take care of you. Now let's try and find what we came here for. We are vampires and should not be ashamed of our uniqueness. Deer are for mortals to dine on."

"Lilith, that uniqueness almost got us beheaded in London! We must be more careful here."

"Of course! And that is why I chose here instead of China. They are more savage here than in the orient or European countries. And what is the best about living here is that no other human on earth knows these savages exist since this land is an undiscovered territory. We will be able to exist here without the fear of exposure." Lilith said with a toothy grin.

"It seems like all talk on your part so far, Lilith. Not one whiff of a mortal's blood has passed my nose. And need I remind you that we are on day two of hunting in this hellhole! It took us several weeks to get here, and we couldn't feed off the crew from the only ship willing to take us in. I am beyond famished, darling. So the deer look quite appetizing at this point to me."

"You are just weak, my dear. That will all change the minute we come across—" Lilith's voice trailed as she looked off into the distance. "Do you smell that?"

"Yes. It's putrid. It smells like wet wool!"

"Perhaps, but there's a slight undertone to it."

"Yes! You are right! There's a faint scent of patchouli."

"And also the faint stench of human perspiration. We have found the savages, darling!"

The two raced off in the direction of the scents and came upon Zhang, Chief Strongbow, Keme, and Chepi within a few minutes. The vampires took to the shadows to observe their marks.

"I only saw two in my vision, Chief Strongbow, but I cannot be certain that more will not follow. I sensed that one of them has a respectful—shall we say—following?"

"It would stand to reason that these two would bring forth more of their kind once they found comfort here. But I still cannot fathom how we will stop this. You said we mortals are weak against the vampires. How will just you, Keme, and Matchitehew be able to fend these immortals off? And granted--that's if Matchitehew has mastered his power of the wolf. I personally fear he will go rogue."

"You will not like his answer, Chief," Wisakachek said as he appeared from the brush.

Chief Strongbow's eyes widened as he saw the god Keme described walk toward him, and then

Strongbow bowed before him. "Great god of the wolves, forgive me, but what exactly do you mean by that?"

"Chief, it is the destiny of the strongest in the Fox and Sauk tribes to be made into wolves. Only they can defeat these immortals."

"Forgive me again, but I do not understand."

"He's the god that made Keme and Matchitehew into wolves, Strongbow, and now he wants to make more warriors out of your tribes. It's the only way to defeat a vampire's strength. For they have the strength of 20 men." Zhang interrupted.

"That is correct, Zhang."

"Wisakachek, it has been a while," Zhang said.

"Yes, it has. Too long! What's it been now? 30 moons since I saw you last?"

"I believe so."

"If what you both are saying is the will of the gods, why now? Why did we not possess the power of the wolves before this? It will take my people some time to harness such greatness, and I fear there is little time to prepare for these immortals." Said Chief Strongbow.

"You are correct in thinking that the time to prepare yourselves against the vampires is limited." Said Wisakachek.

"That word hasn't crossed the lips of any soul since long ago. My great, great grandfather spoke of such creatures. He also believed they were death walking among the living."

"THEY KNOW we are here already, Drake."

"Yes, but it seems they fear they cannot overcome our powers."

"True, and that notion can help us when we hunt them, but we should still study them for a bit before we track them for the kill."

"Lilith, how often have I told you to stop playing with your food?"

"I do no such thing!" Lilith hissed while slapping Dracula's shoulder. "I merely want the chase and the hunt to be as exhilarating as the actual kill. Is that too much to ask?"

"Perhaps not, especially since we know very little about that one and the god," Drake said as he motioned to a large black wolf coming out of the forest.

"Keme! How are you, my good man!" Said Wisakachek.

Keme transformed into his human form.

"Let's all talk in the village. We will need the help of the other strong warriors to defeat these vampires." Wisakachek said.

Lilith and Dracula watched them walk off toward the village until they all disappeared from sight.

"What do you think they are planning?"

"What does it matter, Drake? Whatever they think they have to defeat us will never be strong enough. Sure, they have that sorcerer and some type of human shifter. But how much damage can they inflict on the two of us together? We are both strong, quick, and possess just as much knowledge of dark arts as that sorcerer does." She protested.

"You may be right, but— "

Lilith let out a sigh. "You won't let go of finding a deer to feast on, will you? Let's find one if that pleases you. Then we can get back to tracking these savages and see what they have planned."

"That pleases me greatly, my darling." He said as he stroked her cheek and chin with his thumb.

"Hunting with you gets me excited for many things." He pressed his lips to hers.

They both darted deep within the forest to hunt for some deer and came upon a buck, a doe, and 2 fawns drinking from a brook within the first few minutes of their hunting.

Dracula smiled as he motioned to Lilith that he was about to pounce upon the family of deer. He sprang out towards the unsuspecting animals and, within seconds, had the buck and doe by the jugular. Lilith followed behind Dracula and had the two fawns in each of her arms.

"It's just like you to go after the harder kill and leave me bored to tears with the weaker ones," Lilith said with a chuckle.

"I am sorry, but after all this talk about hunting, I got excited." He then bit into the buck and suckled on its neck.

"Save a little of him for me, darling! You know how much I like to share!" She said with a sheepish grin.

"And you know how much I like to watch you."

Lilith bent down slowly toward one of the fawns. She dramatically exposed her fangs to give Dracula the show he wanted. She then did the same with the other fawn and dropped them both from her hands once they were drained dry.

"Darling, you know how much this turns me on."

"I'm well aware, Drake," Lilith said as she pulled his torso next to her waist. Her hands cupped each cheek of his backside, pushing his hardened shaft into her inner thigh. "Your body sings for my seduction." She whispered while sliding one of her hands around his thigh and caressing his bulge. "Yes, oh so giving, indeed."

Dracula lowered her corset to expose her breasts. He flicked his tongue over the peak and sucked it briefly before cupping it in his palm. "What can I say, darling? You bring out the best in me." He lowered her body to the ground and hitched up her dress. "I want nothing more than to please every little inch of you." He removed her panties and then slicked his tongue over the inner lips of her slick folds while plunging two fingers inside her. Lilith let out a moan of pleasure and a whimper when he removed his fingers and mouth from her aching, drenched core. He placed his fingers, filled with her sweetness, into his mouth and licked off every morsel. "It appears that your body sings too, my darling. Let's see if I can play with this body enough to produce more of the honey I desire. Shall we?"

"I would like nothing more, Drake."

He lowered the other side of her corset to expose both mounds. His lips grazed the middle of both and then each peak. His mouth trailed towards her stomach and then briefly rested on each inner thigh before settling back on her sex. Lilith writhed beneath Dracula as his tongue flicked and circled her opening. Her breath hitched as he pulled her lips back to slide his tongue deeper within her.

She moaned softly again and ran her fingers through his thick locks. "Drake, my darling, I believe my body is about to crescendo."

Dracula lifted his head from her and stood up. "Then let me tune it for some up-tempo." He removed his pants. "I want you, darling."

"Oh, Drake, I want you too."

Dracula lowered his member near her opening. He thrust himself inside her quickly, and only a short breath escaped Lilith's lips. His thumbs then found her peaks as his cock plunged deep within her core.

"That's it, my darling! Let me play you."

Lilith became unglued beneath him as her juices flowed and her center wrapped around his shaft tightly.

"Yes, my queen! Let yourself go and sing for me."

Lilith let out a loud moan and then collapsed and relaxed after her release of pleasure.

"Don't get too relaxed, darling. I expect an encore." A wry smile appeared on his face before he claimed her lips.

"All the warriors have been chosen, and the battle plan is in place. I suggest we all turn in early to surprise the vampires at dawn." Chief Strongbow announced to both the Sauk and Fox tribes.

Keme started to walk toward his village when Chepi grabbed his arm.

"Can we talk for a minute before you head back to the tribe for rest?"

"Sure. What is it that you want to talk about?"

"Not here." She whispered. "Follow me."

Chepi led Keme to the forest. The two walked until they were at a large rock close to the brook that led to the waterfall near Zhang's cottage.

"Why are we here, Chepi?"

"I want to be with you before you battle with the vampires." She said as she laid her head on his chest.

"I also wanted to hear your heartbeat as a reminder that you are strong and will come back to me in one piece."

"Chepi," he cupped her face and drew her forehead close to his, "nothing will happen to me. Both Wisakachek and Zhang have made me a strong warrior wolf. I am certain I can defeat them."

"Are you totally certain?"

"As certain as my feelings for you are."

Chepi stroked his cheek and drew her lips to his. Their softness made Keme wrap his arms around her and pull her tight. His lips then trailed down toward her chin and searched for her neck. When she let out a breath, his search was complete. He caressed her shoulders while kissing her neck, and then his hands rested on her chest. Opening one side of her dress, he exposed her nipple. Keme let out a hitched breath once his thumb circled it, and it peaked with desire. Chepi released a soft moan and guided Keme's head to her exposed breast. His tongue slicked over the nipple, and then his mouth took hold of her breast.

"Keme, please take me."

His hands slid down her thighs and raised her dress.

"You are so beautiful." He said as he stroked her center. "I want you. Every inch of you." He loosened the tie on his buckskin, dropping it to the ground. His hands found and loosened the ties to Chepi's dress. Keme studied every inch of her curves as the dress slid slowly off her.

Once her dress fell to her feet, he grabbed her backside and pulled her close to his stiff rod. She grabbed his backside in return, and they both rested their bodies on the smooth part of the rock. She straddled him and started to thrust against his member.

"Chepi, not so fast!" Keme said as he tucked her beneath him.

"I want to take you. And I want to pleasure you with a kiss. Let me have a taste of you?" He whispered in an almost inaudible tone as he traced her inner folds with his index finger.

His lips trailed from her ear and brushed her neck, shoulders, breasts, torso, and stomach before reaching their desired destination. His tongue slicked over the outside of her opening while he thrust his index and middle finger into her center.

Chepi let out a moan and reached for his shoulders. Once her hands found the broadness of his shoulders, she dug her nails into his skin as she writhed beneath him. He then raised himself and thrust his rod deep within her as his hips rocked in unison to hers.

"You are a perfect fit, Chepi." He said as he caressed her cheeks. She let out another moan as her hips bucked at a faster pace.

A rush of heat surged through Keme's body as he

found himself bucking in unison to her speed. Chepi wrapped her hands around his backside and pulled him close. His hands found her breasts, and he started to caress them until the nipples pebbled. She began to thrust faster to his touch. He found himself wanting nothing more than to release inside her.

He raised his torso to watch her body move with unbridled, excited pleasure and then found one of his fingers trailing down toward her clit. His thumb traced it while thrusting himself deep into her. Her womanhood, wet with excitement, wrapped tighter around his shaft, and a moan escaped her lips.

Keme continued to gyrate quickly until he released inside of her. After taking several breaths, he collapsed on top of her and wrapped his arms around her neck.

"I am very much in love with you, Chepi."

"I love you too."

"No, you do not understand. I cannot live another moment without you as my bride. I want to marry you, my sweet."

"It would be a great honor to be your wife, Keme. Promise me something?"

"Anything, my love." He said, stroking her cheek.

"Promise we will wed the minute you return from battling the vampires?"

He stroked her cheek again and tousled her hair. "That, my love, I can promise you." He stood up and extended his hand to her. "Come! Let us tell our people this good news. I believe it will strengthen their bond with one another, so we are further prepared to battle."

"Are you certain the change in the Warriors has occurred already?"

"Yes. Wisakachek said that it should not take long. The moon is full and high now. We should be able to hunt for the vampires shortly."

"Didn't Wisakachek say they would be strongest at night?"

"These two, according to Zhang, are strong in both the light of day and night. The female was made like me. Her power is greater than any others like her. Zhang was not sure how the other one came to his powers, but he believed that there was a strong possibility that he was somehow made himself. All Zhang knows is that the male is well versed in the dark arts."

Once they finished dressing, they returned holding hands and were greeted by Chief Strongbow and Zhang when they arrived.

"Father, we have news to share."

"I trusted that you might. And even though I still do not regard this as a wise choice for you, my daughter," he started while looking at Keme, "I believe that this is the will of the gods. You both have my blessing!" he continued as he put his arms around them both. "Come! Let us tell our people of this good news."

Chief Strongbow gathered both tribes and announced his daughter's engagement with the help of Keme's father, the Sauk Chief. Within minutes both tribes greeted the couple with hugs and kisses of approval.

"This is a great day for both of our tribes! The gods have chosen to make us unite out of love! The two wish to be joined together immediately after the battle with the vampires."

An enormous cheer rumbled throughout the sea of warriors and tribes, and everyone started to dance. Keme's father placed his hands on his son's and soon-to-be daughter-in-law's shoulders and quickly hugged them both before joining in dance with the rest of the joined tribe.

EIGHT

Lilith put her hand on the giant oak tree beside her to steady herself as she and Dracula observed the tribes preparing for a battle with them.

"I'm certain we no longer have a choice, Drake. The element of surprise is gone. We must attack now while they are not expecting us to."

"I have a bad sense about this, darling. A real bad one."

"You heard them! They are planning to attack us at dawn! They have one shifter and one sorcerer. The rest are humans. How much trouble could that be?" Lilith said as she leaped out into the clearing for the attack without another hesitation.

She went straight for Chief Strongbow's jugular, and he fell limp in her hands within seconds of the confrontation, completely drained of blood. Lilith took on a few of the front-line warriors within the next few seconds of battle, and they also proved to be no match for her cunning nature.

Lilith's gaze met Chepi's next, and a smile bore on her lips as she lunged in Chepi's direction. Keme stood in front of Chepi to shield her from Lilith's fangs. Once Lilith came within a foot of Keme, he transformed into his dire wolf form. Matchitehew and two other warriors from the Fox tribe followed Keme's lead by shifting into their own wolf forms.

Dracula sucked in a breath as he watched in horror the four wolves transforming before him. He lunged into the fight, hoping to save Lilith from the now unfair odds. The sorcerer stepped in front of Dracula just before he reached Lilith and waved his staff, causing Dracula to be shoved into a nearby oak tree. His head wrapped against the tree's girth, making Dracula close his eyes to squelch the searing pain in his head.

Holding the crown, he shook the pain out of his head. When his eyesight cleared, his gaze fell upon Lilith's. The four wolves were scratching and pulling at Lilith's extremities. Dracula targeted the first two that were tearing into Lilith's shoulders, and with a wave of his hand, they hurled through the air. He then deflected the other two ripping into her thighs with another wave of his hand.

After deflecting all four wolves, Dracula scooped Lilith up, and a green mist started forming around them. The fog consumed the two, and they disappeared from sight.

CHEPI RAN towards her father and lifted his limp body. Tears welled in her eyes and streamed down her cheeks as she drew his body near her lap. She let out a shrilling cry after she gently closed his eyes. Keme rushed to her before the rest of the village gathered around her.

"This is not how I pictured this battle to end, nor is it how I pictured my wedding day, Keme," Chepi said as she sucked in the air between each word. Her tears became violent.

"I know, my love." He put his hand on her shoulder and knelt beside her.

"But even though it is not how I pictured it, we must continue with our plans. My father would have wanted that." She stroked her father's hair and kissed his forehead.

"Chepi, you need time to mourn. So do our people." Keme whispered in her ear as his hands blanketed both of her shoulders.

"Then we all mourn, but only for one day. Father would not want us shedding any more tears than necessary for him. He never wanted anyone to make a fuss over him. We can marry each other tomor-row." She said as she cupped his cheek. "Besides, I couldn't wait longer than a moon to be your wife."

"If that is what you wish, my love, then we can make it so."

"Yes. That is what I wish."

CHAPTER

NINE

D racula released his tight grip on Lilith enough to examine her wounds. Some were superficial around her arms and would heal within a day or two, but the others deep and close to her neck would take far longer. Her body limped weakly in his arms as he examined her for more wounds around her legs.

He shed a blood-stained tear when he saw the exposed bone on her right thigh.

"Oh darling, I told you I had a bad feeling about this. I almost lost you today." He said as he stroked her hair.

"It is alright, Drake. I just need a little time and some Dark Sleep."

"I don't ever want to exist without you." He said as he kissed her forehead. "We are going back to England. And I don't want any arguments from you.

I will find a suitable sewer for your Dark Sleep." He said as he pulled her close to his chest. A green mist formed around them again, and within minutes they were on the outskirts of London, England.

"You will be better soon, darling. I promise you that." He said as he moved her into the shadows of the woods to a nearby cemetery. "I'll look for a beggar tonight. They have no human ties and won't be missed."

"Beggars carry a stench. It spoils the taste." She said as she shrugged her shoulders and pouted her lips.

"Do not argue with me, darling. You are weak and in need of blood. I won't be long. Wait for me here."

"Oh, Drake, you are always trying to take care of me. It's such a sweet thing." She said as her shaking finger met the tip of his nose.

"And I always will take care of you. It's my duty to care for my Queen." He said as he took her hand into his and kissed it gently before mist encompassed his body, and he disappeared.

Lilith tried to lift her torso up so she could assess her wounds but found it hard to will her body to move the way she pleased. She let out a whimper when she adjusted her body enough to view the deep wound in her right thigh.

Dracula materialized again with a foul-smelling beggar as an offering in his arms.

"I have brought him to you, my darling."

"Thank you, Drake. You are too kind." Lilith snapped her index finger and thumb, and the beggar instantly gazed at Lilith in a trance-like state.

The man removed his bulky coat and leaned his neck towards Lilith. She traced his chest with her index finger and slit his thin soiled tee shirt with her nail from the neckline to the bottom. She then found the strength to straddle the man and opened the slashed shirt to expose his chest.

"This kind man told me you are the Queen, and I am here to serve you, Your Highness." The beggar said. His voice was monotone.

"Oh, darling, you will serve me well!" Lilith said as she traced the man's exposed chest with her index finger.

Dracula reached for her free hand and kissed her palm.

"You know how much I like to watch, right, darling?"

"Oh yes, Drake. I know exactly how much." She tugged on the top of her corset to expose her breasts. She placed Drake's hand on her breast, and he caressed each nipple with his palm as she squeezed the torso of the man beneath her. "And I love it when you do."

She then lunged for the man's chest cavity with her mouth and bit down into it. Her teeth and tongue quickly met his heart, and the man limped into a quiet death within seconds. She then drained him of all of his blood and stood up.

"I see you are feeling better," Dracula said as he stood up to meet her lips.

"Yes, I am. I may need a few more people like him, but for now? I feel much better." She said as many of her wounds started to heal instantaneously.

"Better enough for me to please you?" Dracula cupped both of her breasts and kissed her neck.

"I would very much like to be pleased." She grabbed both cheeks of his buttocks and ground them into her core.

Dracula scooped her into his arms and laid Lilith on a grassy patch near the forest. He then stood up to unbuckle his pants and slid them down to his knees, along with his breeches, where they dropped to his ankles.

"You lay back and relax. Let me pleasure you, darling." He said as he stroked his rod for her to see its erection.

"Oh, darling, I wouldn't have it any other way."

He knelt beside her, untied her corset, and raised her dress enough to lower her undergarments. Lilith winced as Dracula grazed the wound on her thigh that had now formed some tender skin over the bone.

"Perhaps there is a better way to please you." He said as he licked his index and middle fingers. "Yes, I think I have found a better way." He placed his wet fingers onto her clit and caressed the opening until her wetness enveloped them. He then thrust them into her as he kissed each of her breasts.

"I want you, Drake."

"I know, and that will happen in due time when you are stronger. For now, let me pleasure you by having a bite." He whispered as his lips slid from her nipples to her stomach and rested over her opening. He opened her thighs slightly and the lips of her entrance and slicked his tongue over her womanhood. Lilith writhed and moaned beneath him as his mouth engulfed every inch of her opening.

"Oh, Drake! Don't stop!" She pleaded as she thrust herself into his face.

His hands found her backside, and he cupped each cheek in his palms as he drove his tongue deep within her. She grabbed the back of his head and tousled his hair while grinding herself into his lips. She then let out a few breaths in between some moans.

"I'm coming, baby. I'm coming for you!" She screamed.

Dracula thrust three of his fingers into her opening as he continued to lick and suck on her clit. He continued to grind his fingers into her until cool wetness flushed his face and fingers. He lifted his head from her opening, smiled once his gaze met hers, licked his lips, and sucked on his fingers.

"I knew I'd find a suitable way to please you, darling." He said with a toothy grin.

Lilith tapped him on the nose with her index finger.

"Yes, you certainly found a suitable way."

Dracula redressed Lilith and himself and scooped her into his arms. Her head pressed against his chest, and she kissed him lightly. Dracula's body spun into a tornado-like funnel, and the earth swelled around their bodies until they were hidden from any mortal's view. They were now protected from everyone and everything that might cause them harm while they entered the Dark Sleep.

TEN

The sun peeked through the opening of the teepee, signifying that the day had arrived. All the village women rushed over to help Chepi dress in a beautiful milky white colored buckskin dress with layers of fringe around each arm that draped down to the ground. The mid-section framed her waist with a colonial blue belt beaded with bone and silver medal. Her moccasins mirrored the dress with milky white fringe, and a blue leaf was sewn onto the top of each throat line. The oldest woman of the tribe helped Chepi put on the manta beads.

Chepi headed out of the teepee and walked over to the cornmeal the women collected for her. She started grinding it, hoping that act would burn wonderful memories into her now clouded and heavy mind.

Ever since she had met Keme, she had dreamed of marrying him, but there was sadness that surrounded her happiness, too, since her father would not be there to watch her unite both the Sauk and Fox tribes in love.

"We knew this day would come for you soon, Chepi. The women and I made you this for the ceremony." Chepi's Aunt said as she folded an intricate triangle wheel-patterned blanket around Chepi's shoulders. "We started making it for you since you became a woman in the tribe. I hope you like the colors."

Chepi maneuvered the blanket towards her eyes so she could see the brown, green, blue, red, and white colors intermixing and forming an integrating pattern of unity. Chepi blinked back a tear that started as she meditated on the symbolism of unity the blanket had for both her love for Keme and the love that both tribes would have for each other.

"It is beautiful! Thank you so much!" Chepi said as she pulled the blanket closer to her.

"Come! Let's find this husband of yours!" Her Aunt said while catching a stray tear that tried to escape from her cheek. "We must present him with your ground meal!"

Chepi took step after step in the village, and it seemed like the trip to Keme was longer than usual. Keme greeted Chepi with a smile.

"You look beautiful, my love."

"And you are handsome."

"Alright, you two! Sit down so I can wash your hair!"

The Aunt tirelessly worked on washing the couple's hair and then braided a few strands together.

"There! You are now ready to pray together to the rising sun."

Keme took both of Chepi's hands.

"I cannot believe you will soon be my wife. This is a great miracle to have you in my life, Chepi. I love you with all of my soul and promise to love and protect you as long as we are together." Keme said to her as his lips pressed her thumbs.

"There will be plenty of time for that later! You have a rising sun fast approaching the horizon. It's time to pray." The Aunt said as she forced the two out into the village. "Go now to the brook. We will all see you shortly." She said to them both while kissing the backs of their heads.

Keme and Chepi walked towards the brook, hand in hand. When they were at the stream, they knelt before the rising sun and prayed until it lifted high into the morning sky.

"We, along with our people, are now one, my love," Keme said as he touched her forehead with his.

Chepi smiled and pressed her lips against his cheek.

"Yes, that we are."

The two slowly walked back to the village to celebrate their marriage with their newly joined tribe.

THE END

BEFORE YOU GO...

Enjoyed the book? You can sign up for my newsletter where I offer more fun!

I promise I won't bombard you with tons of emails! I generally write them once a week or once a quarter depending on my writing schedule!

https://www.authoramandakimberley.com/newsletter-signup

RESEARCH

Research Websites:

http://www.sacandfoxks.com/sacfox.nsf/ContentPage.xsp?action=openDocument&documentId=EC854C1650666A8B862576950079CFE2

http://kentuckywerewolves.weebly.com/original-write-up.html

https://en.wikipedia.org/wiki/History_of_Native_Americans_in_the_United_States

http://www.lancasterarchery.com/blog/a-basic-guide-to-the-parts-of-a-bow/

https://en.wikipedia.org/wiki/History_of_the_Romani_people

http://shop.hauntedcuriosities.com/Native-American-Werewolf-Totem-82712015.htm

http://www.legendsofamerica.com/na-astronomyculture.html

http://www.native-languages.org/legends-night.htm

https://www.manataka.org/page348.html

IF YOU LIKED FOREVER CHERISHED YOU MIGHT LIKE...

MIDNIGHT & MISTLETOE

USA TODAY BEST SELLING AUTHOR

AMANDA KIMBERLEY

MIDNIGHT & MISTLETOE

CHAPTER ONE: NEW BEGINNINGS

Priya tried to braid her hair again for the fourth time, but she still couldn't get the frizz fest to behave itself.

"It's no use. I'm going to have to jump in the shower and drench it."

It was the first day of her new life, and everything had to be perfect since she'd be working with *"the"* Braden Boss, a highly successful chef with his own TV show on The Food Channel. She wasn't horribly keen on having had to use her womanly wiles on the man to get the job, but her daddy always said, 'If you've got it, flaunt it.' And her triple D cup size surely became a definitive flaunting mechanism with this man.

Three years ago, she wouldn't have had to stoop so low to allow her physical features to speak for her successes. Her money and fame in the business world made her a respected woman back then. But now, after everything she'd suffered, including her own dignity ripped from her, she found herself starting over. Sadly, she had less than when she was fresh out of college, which proved to be the worst low of her life. Because now? Now she needed to be content with playing second fiddle as a sous-chef to one of the most famous culinary brilliants in the business today. Not that she couldn't share the spotlight. She was good at that, but given what she knew about Boss, he wouldn't share it—he'd hog it.

The braid finally took shape after she drenched her hair, and she secured it with a hair tie before she let out a tremendous sigh.

"Please, my dear Lord, let me get through today with little to no problems. It will be bad enough to swallow my pride for the next 10 hours because the last thing I need is an ogling boss or a botched dinner."

She put on a little foundation, blush, and mascara—not wanting to look as if she just came off the runway since what she had on was distracting enough. The man—at least during the interview proved incorrigible, only hiring her for her perky assets, so she didn't need to prove him right by gussying herself up to the nines. He never looked north of her chest during the hour-long interview. That alone convinced her the tabloids had been right. He was a billionaire bad-boy who only had a serious relationship with his coffee maker. Of course, she had something in common with his Keurig. The man knew how to push her buttons.

She grabbed her purse and keys and headed out the door. The drive to The Odd Duck wasn't far from her apartment via the highway. But come winter, she'd have to leave her house two hours early during a snow "storm" to use the back roads if she had any hopes of getting there on time. Southerners weren't exactly known for being able to drive in inclement weather. Two inches of snow here would compare to a blizzard up in New England—at least according to her cousins from New York City. Texas though? They shut everything down because they can't treat the highways with massive car pileups. And she was not looking forward to January and February, which were only a few short weeks away. It was almost unheard of to land a job in the restaurant field so close to the holidays.

Sure, waitstaff positions were always open, but typically not management. Not that Priya needed the money for Christmas gifts, most of her family was long since buried. Still, since her divorce, she made it a point to look forward to treating herself with a lavish Christmas gift. She felt she deserved it after the hell her ex put her through, and she wasn't going to back down on such a thing this year. It was the first year she could use money from a paycheck instead of her bank account, and she would take pride in herself for accomplishing so much in such little time. She knew no one else at her age that had to start over. Sure, some people go back to school and change careers after retirement, but she was far from her golden years, and she wasn't about to live off her dividends alone. No. She wanted a sense of accomplishment just like anyone else did in their barely thirties did.

She found a parking space a lengthy distance away from the restaurant under a streetlight and pulled in. Once she turned the car off, she let out a long breath to steady her nerves before opening the door. This was like her first job-first day jitters all over again. She slowly placed both feet on the ground and locked her car, trying to stamp out some of her nerves before proceeding toward the entrance. Her stomach did a few backflips as she tried to put one foot in front of the other to make it to the door.

Once through the threshold, a hostess greeted her. Her eyes were half-mast and sunken in, and the hap-hazard eyeliner she applied appeared as if it was from the night before. The bags under her eyes were the most prominent feature of her pale face. She looked overworked and overloaded. Priya scanned the restaurant to see if the rest of the staff was just as tired and most likely hungover, and to her astonishment, it appeared they all were. This was clearly something she needed to change if the place was ever going to appear upscale and profes-sional. The Odd Duck wasn't a chain restaurant with a revolving door of employees. It was established with the intent of being a leading dining experience from ingredients provided by local farmers.

The minute she knew she was interviewing with Boss, Priya began dreaming about Michelin Stars—not that The Odd Duck was even thinking about upscale. They started out humbly like any other restaurant with an unusual yet awesome goal. They only used ingredients from local farmers so they could provide a local unique experience, something Priya could get behind. Now that he had hired her, she wanted the best recognition she could get for the restaurant and for Brayden. Priya cleared her throat, plastered her biggest Southern smile, and asked where the boss was. The hostess's eyes widened.

"We don't call Mr. Boss 'the boss.'" She said with air quotes. "He absolutely hates that. Just a fair warning since this is your first day, Ms.?"

"Priya Pant, but please, call me Priya! I'm not one for such formalities among adults I work with." She bounced out the words as she extended her hand to the hostess, whose lips seemed to thin to nonexistence by the minute. The woman, who wasn't much older than Priya, flicked her eyes to the extended hand and then back to Priya's gaze.

"Um, you might want to rethink what you've got

going on as a first impression. Because the formality of your name is about the only thing respected around here. Again—fair warning. Come on. I'll show you to the kitchen." She said as she turned on her heel and motioned for Priya to follow.

Priya lowered her hand and frowned. She was barely in the door and was already having one of the worst days of her life.

Who doesn't shake hands? Clearly, none of them here! That needs to change.

Priya sucked in a breath as the hostess opened the door to the kitchen. She then motioned for Priya to walk in. Priya's brow furrowed as the hostess turned to walk away.

"Aren't you going to take me to Mr. Boss?"

"Hell no! I stay as far away from the kitchen as I can. No offense, lady? But good luck to you! Maybe I'll see you outside for a smoke break. We like to have bitch sessions out there. Of course, that's if you survive that long."

Priya narrowed her eyes. "I don't smoke."

The hostess laughed loud and long. It almost sounded like a cackle.

"Well, you may not be a smoker now, but I predict you probably will start up soon! Mr. Boss isn't exactly the easiest person to get along with. I figured I'd give you a fair warning since you didn't figure that out from my candor at the door."

Priya shook her head at the clearly deranged

woman. There was little she could do to fix the girl's attitude this early in her sous-chef career at The Odd Duck, but she vowed she'd try. She sucked in a long breath and headed into the kitchen.

A loud clanging filled the air, followed by a mouth so foul she wondered if the vegetables were still fresh.

"Son of a bitch! This sauce tastes like absolute ass! A five-year-old can do better! Make it again, God damn it! And this time—season it before you put that shit in the pan! You graduated from Cornell, for Christ's sake! I expect the best from you, for fuck's sake!"

Priya palmed her reddening cheeks. In all her years of growing up as a minister's daughter, no more than two swear words passed her daddy's lips. And now, her new employer, Braden Boss, said more explicit remarks in two minutes than she had ever heard in her entire lifetime.

Jesus, Mary, and Joseph! What have I gotten myself into?

Braden looked up from the now crying young prep woman and locked his eyes on Priya.

"Thank God you are here! At least someone with an ounce of talent can help me with this fucking train wreck!" He said as he tossed his hands in the air. "Come with me to my office, and we'll go over some itineraries for today's specials. After that, I will have you work with Ms. Fucking Prima Donna right here, so my recipes come out the way I intended them to and not with an added flavor spin that sucks monkey balls. The only way for this restaurant to succeed is for everyone to fucking execute the dishes properly!" He said this in a low growl through gritted teeth before motioning Priya to another area of the kitchen with a door.

Priya stood frozen in her stance. Her knees locked as she tried to will them to move. She did not know that she'd be walking into *Hell's Kitchen* with the Devil reincarnate as her boss, but Priya did get a few things as she was willing her feet to think for themselves. First, she had to force her legs to walk fast because he was already halfway across the kitchen in two strides. Two, she would not give this heathen the satisfaction of watching her burn under the collar. And three, paying for the roof over her head depended on her compromising with this Lucifer. Daddy always taught her about signing her soul away. But clearly, Daddy never met *the* Boss that could accomplish that just by signing her paychecks.

Somehow, somehow, she could put one shaking foot in front of the other and make it to his office.

"Shut the door." He motioned to her as she stepped through it.

He locked on her eyes, but as soon as she sat down in the empty seat opposite him, his eyes went south. Priya frowned at the gesture. Sure, she stooped to a new level of stupid with getting hired, but that didn't mean she had to take his ogling daily at work. He should be more of a professional gentleman, but clearly—he didn't get the memo.

"So, Ms. Perky, let's talk about the specials for today." He said with a smile, eyes still locked on her chest.

Priya bent down slightly in her chair to meet his gaze and waved a hand in front of his eyes.

"Hi. First off, my eyes are north of where you are looking. Second, it's Priya—not perky." She said as she crossed her arms over her chest.

It didn't do much to cover up her enormous triple-D cups, but she certainly didn't want to get the attention she had been in his office for the last few minutes.

He chuckled.

"Whatever you say, Ms. Perky."

Priya let out a huff.

Braden cleared his throat and lowered his gaze to the floor before continuing. "Sorry, Ms. Priya. So, let's get down to business and pick from these four for today's and tomorrow's specials. I was thinking either quail stuffed with fresh figs and prosciutto or quail in rose petal sauce for the first choice and for the second either smoky citrus butter-baked redfish or mustard-maple roasted salmon." He said as he spread some notes onto the desk in front of her. His fingertips brushed her hand slightly as she reached for one page of notes and an electric heat surged through the tips of her fingers that traveled right down to her core.

There was no denying that Braden was attractive with his luscious dark and wavy locks and chestnut brown eyes. His solid forearms and citrus, musky scent drove her to the point of insanity too. But no amount of crazy would be worth an attraction to the foul-mouthed buffoon. She shook her head in protest of her body's reaction and crossed her legs to stop her libido from singing any amount of praise to the gorgeous god before her. He was her employer, and that was that.

"Well, my specialty is Italian and Southern foods. I'd love to work with the prosciutto and fig recipe because it sounds fun and flavorful. As far as the fish goes—wild salmon is in season now through August, so we should take advantage of the mustard-maple recipe. Even the maple syrup will be delicious now because it is also in season. The redfish recipe sounds mouth-watering, but I'd wait till August for that one. Perhaps we can do smoked citrus for a salmon dish for tomorrow instead?"

Braden smiled from ear to ear. "Apparently, I was right about you being sharp. I threw in the red herring—or in this case—the redfish to see if you knew what was seasonal. I've always found fish should be in season for a perfect meal because it just tastes better." His eyes met hers for the first time since they walked into his office, and she could see they were twinkling with delight as he talked about food. It was the first time he appeared human instead of a horny bastard.

"I know we talked briefly in the interview, but I never got to ask what your favorite dish is to prepare."

He was clearly searching, and Priya was tongue-tied. No man should look that gorgeous! It should be a crime against humanity. Of course, his potty mouth left much to be desired, and she focused on that to get the wheels in her brain to move. Still, what could she possibly say to impress this famous chef?

"Well, in all honesty, it would have to be manicotti." She blurted out the statement almost without thinking it over. She drew out her pronunciation of manicotti in an Italian/New York/Southern drawl. "My grandma made them from scratch every Thanksgiving, and I make them on special occasions in her memory. I do the same with lasagna, too—even though she didn't make that as much."

His eyes brightened again. He got up from behind his desk and reached out to cup Priya's cheeks. Priya shot up from her chair. Sure, she thought the guy was a hornball, but she never thought he'd touch her this brazenly in his own office, at which any point someone could enter. They were nearly a breath apart, and Priya sucked in as much air as she dared through her slightly parted lips. He couldn't know he had this effect on her because she wouldn't allow it.

"Priya, I didn't care about the dish you'd tell me. All I cared about was the passion behind it. I knew my gut was right about hiring you." He said while he pressed his lips on both of her cheeks and made a soft smacking sound. They were so buttery smooth, and she barely realized he was kissing her until he met her gaze again. She tried to recoup her look of horror, but she wasn't doing very well in hiding it. "Sorry! I don't mean to make you uncomfortable. It's just that you remind me of my family. They were all chefs and all from Europe. I'm sure you know it's customary to greet each other by kissing cheeks."

"Really? You didn't care about the dish?" She found her hands cupping both of his that still cradled her face. She blinked a second longer than she needed to as Priya moved into his touch, but only slightly before she corrected herself. *He's your boss, Priya! Stop panting over him!* "And no, the European greeting isn't uncomfortable for me. I'm literally second-gen off of the boat. My grandparents were the first to arrive here off Ellis Island. After growing up in my family and spending a summer abroad, I'm used to the warm welcome in Italy and Spain. My dad's side has been here far longer. He's from India originally." Her eyes widened at her own realization of surprise and shock intermixing her feelings at his gesture. She didn't want such closeness with the man because of who he was, yet her body hummed the instant he touched her.

"Yes, my family is mostly from Europe and mostly Italy, though I have some India descent in my family tree on his side, too." He said as he lowered his hands and placed them in the pockets of his skin-tight black jeans.

God, how she wished to be those hands touching his skin through that thin layer of fabric on his thighs. *Priya! Don't, girl! It's barely an hour into your first day!*

"Sounds nice. Mine were mostly from Italy, too."

"I wish I could have them here for the holidays. Unfortunately, they are all deceased."

"I'm sorry to hear that. It's always hard when our loved ones have passed. I've had my fair share of family members dying these past few years, too. There aren't that many of mine left either. I've got some cousins on my grandfather's brother's side, and that's the side from India. But that's about it."

"Yes, and sadly, you can't do anything except live on without them."

"True." Priya lowered her gaze.

Not knowing what more to say, she quickly changed the subject. This was the first time she met and connected with her boss, and she'd be damned if she screwed this up. She had to get him to like her; talking about dead relatives would not cut it.

"So, have we decided on quail stuffed with prosciutto and figs?"

"I think so. Come back to the kitchen, and I'll show you how I make and plate it." He said as he patted her shoulder and smiled.

Another wave of energy surged through her body as his hand patted her shoulder, and she swore her stomach did a backflip.

They both worked in relative silence in large part in the now all too massive kitchen for the first few minutes as they diced up some onions and garlic. To Priya's surprise, it was an extremely comfortable quiet between them. Usually, when getting to know a coworker, she'd fill the time with idle chat, but this time was different. She didn't feel a need for it. He didn't swear up a firestorm as he had earlier in the morning, which was a welcome relief. But he didn't talk all that much either. However, he did tower over her shoulder as she seasoned the quail with salt and pepper on her cutlery board. She wasn't one to use more than the pinch her ancestors told her to use. Sure, some of them would argue as she grabbed the seasoning between her fingers. But in the end, they all seemed to celebrate once she gingerly salted and peppered her meal. A rush of heat shot through her as he gently tapped her on her forearm.

"Very good. Now rub the meat with this herbal poultry mix and butter like this." The tone was as soft as the touch of his hands over hers.

"Make sure you get every curve—I mean cranny. Rub every part of that thing, so it browns well."

She laughed internally after she let out a shaky breath. Clearly, she wasn't the only one moved by the love they were making in this kitchen.

Priya! Stop it, girl. No sexy thoughts while you make food!

"Yes, sir." She had to say something and thought it was best to jest with a cheeky smile.

"Here," He handed her the figs and prosciutto to place inside the bird's cavity.

His hand grazed hers again, sending another course of electric heat through her arm and traveling straight to her core.

"Thanks." She directed her gaze at the bird in a desperate attempt to avoid eye contact.

"That looks beautiful."

"Thanks. I think it looks good, too."

"The quail?" He whispered in her ear as he bent over her.

"Yes, the quail. What did you think I meant?" She asked as heat rushed to her cheeks when she turned to meet his gaze.

His lips turned into a broad smile.

"I'm asking if you could pass me the quail so I can place it in the oven, but if you must know, that dish isn't the only beautiful thing in this kitchen."

She swallowed hard before handing him the dutch oven that contained the quail, and he placed it in the oven. She quickly busied herself with chopping some lettuce for the side salads they were pairing with the quail.

The aroma of the quail browning beautifully in the oven touched their noses after an hour of baking. Braden pulled them out and smiled as he turned to her.

"Smells and looks like perfection." He said while he made up a plate. "I'll leave you to plating yours as I have shown you here." He said as he started wiping his hands. "You can sample these since this was a practice plate. I'll catch you before the dinner rush. I have a taping to do for the show and will be out for the rest of the afternoon."

Priya smiled at him briefly before getting to work on plating the dish. She watched him leave the kitchen. It was bittersweet to see him go because even though his backside was genuinely exquisite, she had to admit that a part of her wanted him to stay. Cooking up something a little more with her than just a dish was looking to be more on her menu than she cared to admit to herself. And she blushed at the thought of feeling that way about her boss.

Having spent more time with him proved he wasn't as intimidating of a person as she initially thought he was. Still, she was happy that he wouldn't be breathing down her neck for the next few hours, giving her the freedom to walk about the kitchen without brushing against his hard body.

The back of her neck began to sweat just thinking about how many times his hips touched hers while chopping away. And the reprieve would give her something else. It would be the chance she needed to build a rapport with the others in the restaurant. Especially that crazy hostess and the poor prep chef who was still sulking in a dark corner of the kitchen.

Priya knew she needed to get the employees to see Braden's good side. If they could see that, they might be more cheerful and professional while on the job. And that, and not so much the food, was Priya's focus for this budding restaurant.

Still, her long-term goals would be pointless if she didn't perfect his execution. She looked up from her plate and compared it to his, which looked identical. She was pleased with herself right down to the carefully placed herbal garnish.

"C—can you show me what I did wrong?" Said a shaky voice to her right.

Priya looked up from the plates and saw the woman Braden had yelled at earlier. Her blue eyes were bloodshot and puffy from an apparent marathon crying session. Some of her short black hair clung to her cheeks, which were stained with tears.

"Sure. Why don't you get more quail, and we can start a new batch from scratch? I'm Priya, Priya Pant, by the way."

"Donna. Donna Brightman." Said the woman as she nodded with a weak smile.

Donna looked at what Priya was doing and followed until their plates mimicked each other.

"Perfect, Donna!" Priya said with a smile.

The kitchen door flung open. Braden walked through and headed straight towards them both. He looked at both plates, sampled them both, and nodded approval.

"Thanks for setting Donna straight, Priya."

Donna lowered her head and tiptoed to the prep station in the kitchen's corner to start on the asparagus for the salmon side dish. She let out a sigh. Braden followed Donna with his gaze as she walked over to the cutting board. He shook his head slightly and then turned his eyes to Priya.

"What's wrong with her? She's acting like I killed her cat." Braden said in a loud whisper.

"She's still upset about this morning."

"Why? It was a mistake—she corrected it, and we moved on."

"Braden, do you not remember your tone and all the foul language you used with her this morning?"

"Oh, for Christ's sake! I swear all the time. That's just who I am."

"It's an unbecoming tone for an employer." Said Priya as she frowned and shook her head.

"Oh, please, is Little Miss Prissy Priya going to tell me the error of my ways?"

Braden crossed his arms and puffed out his chest as he chuckled. Priya didn't want a choral repeat of this morning, so she narrowed her eyes and crossed her own arms in retort.

"For your information, my daddy was a preacher, and he taught us we didn't need to swear to get our point across to others. He also taught us not to name-call. You do realize that name-calling is a form of bullying, and you, sir, are acting like a child with all your elementary school comments." Priya let out a puff of breath. She couldn't believe she was sticking up for herself and the employees she and her boss shared this early in the game. But as his eyes softened to amusement levels, she grew angrier. "You know, I really thought I was getting through to you earlier when we were cooking the quail together. I guess I was wrong." She let out another breath. "It's like you've got a Jekyll and Hyde syndrome going on or something."

Braden's eyes widened, and his lips curled up before he let out a chuckle. This one was heartier than his first.

"Wow! I didn't think I hired a true Southern belle. This is going to be interesting." He laughed again before turning on his heel to head towards his office. "Very interesting, indeed. Hopefully, you can keep up with this Texas kitchen heat, Ms. Priya."

"What's that supposed to mean?"

Braden laughed again before closing the door to

his office. She desperately wanted to run after him, giving him more pieces of her mind. The man clearly needed a good tongue lashing because he forgot the manners his momma, bless her heart, taught him. Of all the times she'd used the phrase, this was most likely the first time she was using it out of sympathy for a woman she only knew through the tabloids and media. A regal and proud woman whose eyes lit up with adoration whenever the papzz interviewed her about Brayden as a child. After a few seconds had passed and she slowed her breathing, she decided against following him. The only certainty of an action like that was her getting fired. And now, more than ever, she wanted to keep this job. If for no other reason, she was determined to keep it to show Mr. Bossypants that he couldn't get her goat!

OR YOU MIGHT LIKE...

EQUIPOISE SOLAR SYSTEM SERIES
Laying Claim to the Lion
USA TODAY BEST SELLING AUTHOR
AMANDA KIMBERLEY

LAYING CLAIM TO THE LION

CHAPTER ONE

"This isn't an option, Verena. If you don't want to marry, you have no choice but to find a suitable male to conceive an heir. Jaxson saw to it that the Valet de Chambre isn't in our favor. And after the Battle of Quell, we appear weak."

Tilda stroked Verena's chestnut hair to braid it. She formed four strands to make a sizeable French braid with Verena's dark locks.

"So what do you expect me to do, Tilda? It's not like our planet has any males on it! And with Jaxson taking over almost all the Equipoise solar system, I won't find anyone willing to defy him."

Verena sighed as she turned to meet Tilda's gaze.

"You certainly can't give into Jaxson. He may want you as his queen, but you know mating with him will be a certain sentence to slavery. Not to mention what it will mean for the rest of our pride.

We've always had an option to seek a mate from any planet of our choosing. But if Jaxson gets his way, none of them are safe. We will be forced to only mate with the people of Emir." Said Tilda.

"I would never think of giving in to him. That panther is simply barbaric! But finding a mate who isn't under Jaxson's tyranny will be hard."

"Earth would be your best option. That solar system is several galaxies away and has never heard of Jaxson. But you must be careful there. Many of the humans on Earth can not shift, and what's worse is that most of them do not believe in shifters. The people are primitive, but if you stick to your feminity, you will find a mate in enough time."

Verena frowned and gripped the guild-colored arm of her thrown. She massaged the lion-carved paw that protruded and curled around the bottom of the arm, hoping the gesture would allow her the privilege of perspective.

"Verena, there are some shifters on that planet, and your abilities will allow you to sense they are. However, they are not as advanced as us. Many of the men are as barbaric as Jaxson. Very possessive, very domineering. But some are suitable mates for an heir."

Tilda shrugged her shoulders and peered out the large glass window that overlooked the lush kingdom. Her eyes fixed on the rainforest that was a little past the main village. A rainbow was forming, and

Tilda smiled. That seemed like a good omen, but she also always loved to meditate on them. And with Effeminate's future hanging in the balance, she could use all the meditating she could find.

"That wasn't what was really bothering me. Shifter or not, it really doesn't matter. I just need the man's seed. I'm not going there to find a mate. The Valet de Chambre's decree merely states that we need an heir. Therefore, I don't need to bring home a mate."

Tilda blinked a few times and then gazed into Verena's eyes.

"What do you mean, you aren't going there to find a mate? We need a king. A king will protect us from Jaxson's tyranny."

Verena stood up and narrowed her eyes as she gazed at Tilda and walked past her towards the window. She placed her hands on the sill and looked out at the vast green jungle, farmlands, and stone buildings that made up the planet she had loved and cared for since birth. Verena pointed out toward the stone-engineered buildings that looked like the pyramids of Earth they once helped the Egyptians build.

"Look at all of them. These women are brilliant and strong. They do not need any male to help protect them, nor do they need a male to construct a building for them. We women of Effeminate built a foundation of powerful warriors in our own right, and I will not let one battle determine our downfall."

"Verena, it may have only been one battle, but it was one that killed your parents and extended this war into several hundred cycles. There's also no end in sight. As your general, I think it's wise for us to explore other options to end it. Especially now that the panther shifters have taken over all but two planets in our solar system. It's just us and the planet Tatsu who are not under Jaxson's thumb."

"Jaxson will never overthrow the dragon shifters. He's not powerful enough to defeat Dragon Jilocasin of Tatsu."

"True, but it is only a matter of time where even the Tatsus will be against us. It's not like those overgrown reptiles have been friendly with any warm-blooded cat ever before. None of the treaties apply to them because of how cold-blooded they are. They don't practice diplomacy. All they seem to do is produce law as part of the council without seeing first-hand how that law will affect any planet. No, the only way to fight off Jaxson is if we find some alphas to help us defeat him. Planet Emir won't have a chance against the shifter species of Earth. I just know it. And besides, your own mother believed in the value of having a male mate from the planet Earth. Having a partner gives you perspective when leading your great people."

Tilda placed her hand on Verena's shoulder. Verena brushed it off.

"Yes, and look at what that value got her! She's dead, Tilda, and so is my father! I can do nothing about that except fight Jaxson without showing weakness. And I believe my father was my mother's downfall. Her love for him was why she fell in battle." Verena crossed her arms and shook her head before continuing, "Her head was too clouded with love. That's why she didn't see that panther coming for her. She was so fixated on the one killing my father. No! I will not allow our sisters to be clouded with love, fear, or apprehension. They don't need to be tied down to a man. They need to focus on this war. We will win the Ebb War and in honor of my mother!" Verena clenched fists. "Now, please prepare my ship for my solo trip to Earth."

"You don't plan on having an escort?"

"What do I need protection from, Tilda? You said it yourself. These shifters are primitive compared to us. I shouldn't need any help with them or finding a suitable seed."

"Yes, my Queen," Tilda bowed before continuing. "How long do you plan on staying so I can better prepare your wardrobe and rations?"

"Not long. An Earth week, perhaps? That should be enough time to find what I need and travel back here in time to challenge Jaxson and the federation's board."

"My Queen, I am uncertain if a week of Earth's time will be enough."

"Doesn't their cycle work like ours?"

"No, it does not. Time is different there. It is hard for me to explain, but you will see a day pass with both light and dark. When it is dark, you will know that a day has passed, and little activity happens until the sun rises the next day. Their moon cycles take 30 days of light and dark."

"But it still sounds like it will take less than a cycle to gain someone with a viable seed."

"I'm sure you are right, my Queen. I will prepare your ship, but are you sure you don't want me to travel with you?"

Tilda brushed some loose strands of Verena's chestnut locks from Verena's cheek.

"You've grown up so fast and so strong, Verena. I understand you may not need me as much as you once did, but you can't blame me for wanting to come and help."

"Tilda," Verena started as she took Tilda's hand, cupping her cheek, and placed it in hers. "You have been the mother I haven't had for many years, and I can't thank you enough for your devotion and love. But I need you here for our planet in my absence. Even though the Valet de Chambre made Jaxson swear to a truce for this whole heir business, I do not trust that he will keep to that promise. Until I am with child, I wouldn't put it past him to attack in my absence. And it would break my heart, as it would yours, to come home to that kind of loss. Please see that our people are safe and continue to train for the next battle."

"Yes, your Majesty. I will."

Tilda bowed her head slightly and smiled as she cupped Verena's face once more.

"And please make sure that you come back to us safely. The Earthlings may be primitive, but that doesn't mean they are tame by any stretch of the means."

"I understand, Tilda."

LAYING CLAIM TO THE LION

CHAPTER TWO

"You must strike while they aren't expecting it, my Liege. The treaty merely states—"

"The treaty merely states that we shall not attack while Verena is looking for a suitor, and I will not break the treaty while she does."

Jaxson beat his fist onto the desk in front of him. It was a light oak plain top with wrought iron legs fashioned in the shape of antlers.

"But Sire, her planet is the only other besides Tatsu that isn't under your reign. And without her and the help of the Effeminate warriors, we could never defeat the dragon shifters on our own. We must strike now while Effeminate is weak."

"Burchard, I will not hear any more of this. I want Verena as my queen, and I cannot have her if we overtake her planet."

"With all due respect, your Majesty, it may be best to take her by force. She's a valiant opponent and should appreciate your strength as a mate."

"I don't want just her respect, Burchard,"

Jaxson's eyes narrowed, and he clenched his fists. Burchard's eyes widened.

"You've fallen in love with the woman, haven't you?"

"That is not your concern, Burchard! Now leave me be so I can look over the strategies you put before me!"

"But Sire, these are strategies for overthrowing planet Effeminate. You just said—"

"I know what I said, Burchard! Now leave me! I have much to think about. Peace treaty or not, we will still resume the war in 30 moon cycles!"

"As you wish, your Majesty."

Jaxson waited for Burchard to close the thick oak door behind him before he let out the breath he was holding in.

What am I going to do? I can't keep denying what I'm feeling. Everyone else knows it. It's not like I'm hiding my attraction to Verena all that well.

Jaxson brushed his fingers through his thick and dark locks and let out a sigh.

It's just that whenever I think of her, she makes me crazy. And if her parents betrothed her to me as they had promised, we wouldn't have had to wage this war. She would have already been mine.

Jaxson let out another breath and pinched the bridge of his nose with his thumb and forefinger.

Great! Another headache! It's all because I've been thinking of her and figuring out how to get her to love me back.

He went over to the window of his meeting room and looked out over the thickly forested area where his people like to hunt. He let out a sigh as he thought about his people trying to take out Verena's pride once more, as they had done during the Battle of Quell.

It was one of the few times his people had come together and fought as one. Before that battle, it proved hard for him to get his people to agree on any common ground. They were all loners and only saw fit to fight when it pleased them. They had never done a thing as a collective before. He even wondered if they would ever do anything as a collective again. Quell was five years ago. And though there were minor battles between Emir and Effeminate since then, those were all minor. Quell was the only major battle fought on Effeminate, and both sides lost a lot of warriors. Emir had fought well and almost won Effeminate, but the other planets in the solar system were easy to take. Their planets had been weak armies, outnumbered, and more self-centered than his people.

The thing was, if he ever had hopes of promising mates to his people, he had to overthrow Verena and planet Effeminate, and somehow this was bothering him. He didn't want to defeat her. He wanted her to reign by his side. Jaxson wished to claim her, take her as his own, to produce an heir that would unite their two kingdoms.

No woman should have to go through life without a mate, just as no man should have to, either. That was the natural order of things on Emir, so he found it challenging to understand Effeminate's all-female planet. Not one lion stayed with a mate on that planet except Verena's mother. Sadly, Verena didn't seem to share her mother's thoughts on companionship.

Still, something had to be done to unite the two planets because a panther-lion shifter would make a new and powerful race. A lion's pride and cunning prowess that could easily lead a battle would serve his elusive and adaptable panthers well, both on the battlefield and in the bedroom. Emir's resources became scarce around the capital. So he knew her lionesses would know precisely what his panthers would need to attain their prey further out in the jungle of their planet. The idea had his heart swelling.

It was still a perfect plan to claim her. And one that Jaxson had been set on since the day he laid eyes on Verena some 364 moon cycles ago when his parents and hers were in peace talks. She was nothing more than a cub like himself, but his territorial cunningness wanted her all to himself, and that was the day he vowed to take her as his own.

Jaxson looked out his window, which overlooked his entire kingdom. He smiled as his eyes gazed upon the thick trees of the land. He used to love climbing them when he was younger, just to think, and Jaxson remembered taking Verena up there when he was a cub. She hated climbing. Of course, no lion likes it. But he enjoyed showing her his world. They shared their first kiss that day, and he hoped to share so much more with her.

He gazed over at the bookshelf that had a picture of the two of them climbing a tree together when they were kids. Jaxson walked over to it and took it down to get a closer look at the prize he intended to claim. As he traced over her picture, he searched to remember what it was like being so close to her body. They only kissed that one time, but it was something that still stuck with him, even after all these moon cycles.

Jaxson let out a sigh.

If only I could get her to see that we are perfect for one another.

He stroked the picture once more and smiled.

I'll talk to her again. Convince her the gods to believe them to be destined mates. And I should do it now, so she doesn't find a mate anywhere else like that stupid law wants her to do. I should be the one to give her an heir. Panthers and lions would be perfect as one!

"Burchard! Prepare my ship! I want to set a course for planet Effeminate tonight."

"Yes, Sire."

ABOUT THE AUTHOR

USA Today Best Selling and award winning author Amanda Kimberley has written in various genres in the course of almost four decades.

Her nonfiction blog, which focuses on the chronic disease fibromyalgia, has garnered recognition from various organizations, including Health Magazine. Naming her blog, Fibro and Fabulous, as a top blog for fibro sufferers.

Amanda has also written for medical magazines

and sites like FM Aware, The National Fibromyalgia Association's magazine and ProHealth.

When Kimberley is not writing nonfiction, she enjoys penning romance. Her first Furry United Coalition story, The Turtle and the Hare, earned the 2020 Summer Splash Book Awards of Ink and Scratches for Best Romance. Her Forever Series Books, Forever Friends and Forever Bound were featured in 2015 and 2016 on the BookCountry website, a division of Penguin/Random House as editor's picks. She has also been featured as a USA Today Happy Ever After Hot List Indie Author with Claiming My Valentine, a Best Poet of the 90's ranking for an anthology, and has had a #1 PNR ranking with Immortal Hunger and Hearts Unleashed.

Amanda Kimberley is a Connecticut native that now lives in the warmth of Northern Texas with her zoo consisting of her husky, tuxedo cat, mice, rabbits, guinea pigs, a tank of fish, two daughters, and a husband.

When she is not writing you can find her cooking whole foods for her pack. She also enjoys reading, hiking, and gaming.

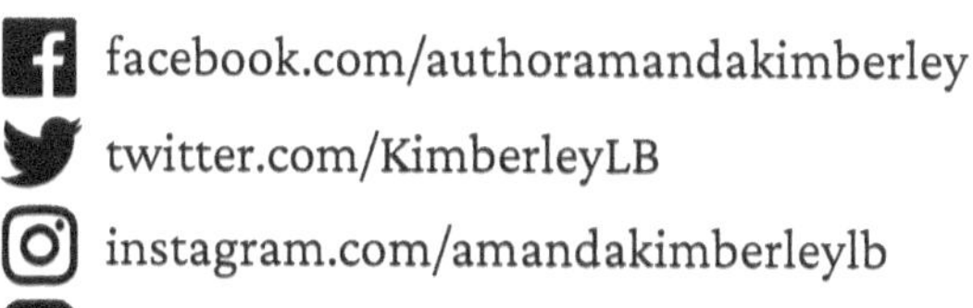

facebook.com/authoramandakimberley

twitter.com/KimberleyLB

instagram.com/amandakimberleylb

tiktok.com/@amandakimberleylb

bookbub.com/profile/amanda-kimberley

ALSO BY AMANDA KIMBERLEY

PNR Series

The Forever Series

Forever Friends

Forever Tied

Forever Cherished

Forever Bound

Forever Immortal

Forever Loved

(Coming Soon)

Forever Blood

(Coming Soon)

Forever Yours

(Coming Soon)

Forever Mine

(Coming Soon)

Historical PNR Series

The Witch Journals Series

Salem's Trial by Judge

Salem's Trial by Township

Salem's Trial by Birth

(Coming Soon)

The Gypsy Witch Trials

(Coming Soon)

Colonial Witch Trials

(Coming Soon)

Stand Alone PNR

The Cure

Manifestations

Uncharted

The Pride Within

Co-Author Stand-Alone PNR

By the Pool with Alex Kimberley

Scifi Fantasy PNR

Suburban Shifter & Celestials Series

Loving the Alpha

Loving the Lone Wolf

Loving the Loup-garou

Loving the Rogue

Loving the Lykos

The Equipoise Solar System Series

Laying Claim to the Lion

Laying Claim to the Legacy

Laying Claim to the Original

Laying Claim to the Dragon

(Coming Soon)

Laying Claim to the Leopard

(Coming Soon)

Laying Claim to the Panda

(Coming Soon)

Laying Claim to the Queen

(Coming Soon)

The Pandemic Series

Pandemic Passion

Pandemic Pandemonium

(Coming Soon)

The Midnight Rising Series

Midnight & Mistletoe

Midnight & Magic

Midnight & Memories

Midnight & Mergers

Midnight & Masquerades

RomCom PNR

The Eve L. Worlds Hellenic Island Shifter Series

The Turtle and the Hare

The Turtle and the Rock

The Ferret and the Fossa

The Leopard and the Llama

(Coming Soon)

Contemporary Romance

The Chronic Collection

Down by the Willow Tree

To Hell With Carpets

Welcome Home

The Chronic Collection

The Just Series

Just Breathe

Just Believe

(Coming Soon)

Just Be

(Coming Soon)

Nonfiction Self Help

The Fibro and Fabulous Series

Fibro and Fabulous: The Book

Fibromyalgia and Sex Can Be a Pain in the Neck

Fibromyalgia and Pregnancy

Poetry

Blue Water Baptism

The Puzzle Called Life

For More Information Please Visit: https://www.bookbub.com/profile/amanda-kimberley